Pilgrims in Love

A NOVEL BY

Frances Beer

inanna poetry & fiction series

INANNA Publications and Education Inc.
Toronto, Canada

Inanna Publications and Education Inc.
212 Founders College, York University
4700 Keele Street
Toronto, Ontario M3J 1P3
Telephone: (416) 736-5356 Fax (416) 736-5765
Email: cws/cf@yorku.ca Web site: www.yorku.ca/cwscf

Interior design by Luciana Ricciutelli
Cover design by Valerie Fullard
Cover art: *Roman de la Rose*, Ms 1126, fol 8r [D 10880]. Photo credit: Dupif Photo Studio. Reproduced with permission. Copyright © Bibliothèque Sainte-Geneviève, Paris

Printed and bound in Canada

Library and Archives Canada Cataloguing in Publication

Beer, Frances
  Pilgrims in love : a novel / by Frances Beer.

(Inanna poetry and fiction series)
ISBN 0-9681290-9-9

I. Title. II. Series.

PS8603.E428P54 2004   C813'.6   C2004-906422-3

for David

Contents

Foreword

The setting of Geoffrey Chaucer's *Canterbury Tales* is a pilgrimage that took place in April, 1387. In his "General Prologue" he describes each of the pilgrims, including a satirical portrait of himself, who participated in this journey from the Tabard Inn near London to the shrine of St. Thomas in Canterbury. It is often said that Chaucer's aim in the *Tales* was to present a microcosm of 14th-century English society; and so his portraits range from the idealistic knight to the ribald miller. The actual tales that Chaucer gives to the various pilgrims were crafted so as to give greater insight into the character of their tellers than could be provided in the "General Prologue" alone.

Like many of his contemporaries, Chaucer was a great borrower and adapter of existing stories. The "Knight's Tale," for example, is based on Boccaccio's "Il Teseida," while the miller's is a combination of a number of comic folk tales. But in each case Chaucer makes the material his own, introducing strategic changes to suit his diverse purposes.

What follows is a re-vision of Chaucer's work, from the point of view of Alison, the Wife of Bath, and Eglentyne, the Prioress. The pilgrims are his, as are the tales they tell—but seen and heard as I believe Alison or Eglentyne would have seen and heard them. I have tried to be true to Chaucer not only in adhering to his descriptions of the pilgrims and their journey, but also by following his custom of creative borrowing. Alison's opening dream, for example, is adapted from Chaucer's own dream vision, "The Book of the Duchess"; her first wedding night is taken from his "Merchant's Tale," as is her third husband's blindness.

While I've expanded considerably, the wife's account of life with her five husbands is based on the details Chaucer provides in the prologue to her tale, and Eglentyne's background corresponds with factual accounts of fourteenth-century conventual life; descriptions of the knight's crusading experiences and of the Black Death are likewise based on historical record.

In filling in some of Chaucer's suggestive blanks I have taken liberties, but my speculations as to the thoughts and deeds of Alison and Eglentyne (as well as several other pilgrims) are inspired by the characterizations that Chaucer provided. Though in their very different ways these two women are notably imperfect, we are allowed to see that many of their faults are attributable to the misogynist world into which they were born, in which they struggled to survive—and we are led to understand and care for them in the course of their respective journeys.

Pilgrims in Love

Bath

The windows were almost as high as the ceiling itself, which was vaulted and ornate as a cathedral or a great palace. They were made of stained glass, the colours rich and varied as a rainbow; the sun shone through them, warming the room, filling it with an array of brilliant hues. Outside the birds sang a hymn of joy to the creation.

I awoke to their song in a bed of incredible softness, the mattress of finest down, the sheets of pure white silk. Drawn towards the harmony of the sun and the birds, I arose and slipped on a gown, also of white silk, that hung by my bed. Outside I found a white palfrey who seemed to await me; I mounted and rode through fields alive with wildflowers and glistening dew, into the wood. I was overcome by pleasure: the softness of the silk against my skin, the song of the birds, the easy motion of the horse beneath me, the colours and fragrance of the fields merging with the darker greens and sweet mossy smell of the wood.

Ahead I was surprised to see a figure in black, seated beneath a tree, in tears. I left my mount, moved quietly towards her, heard her complaint. She was mourning the death of her beloved. We spoke, she told me of her despair, her wish for death. It seemed (or perhaps I wished it so) that her pain was eased as she shared it with me. But as she reached the end of her tale we were interrupted by the sound of a huntsman's horn....

I awoke again, this time to reality. No stained glass, no singing birds, no silken sheets. The April rain was falling outside my ordinary windows, the room was chilly and dark. I was myself again, Alison of Bath, clothmaker, widow (for the fifth time), over forty, with something of a reputation (well-deserved, I must confess) for belligerence and lechery. So I took up my daily routine: breakfast, inspection of my weavers' work, keeping of the books. I was oppressed—not only by boredom, but by my solitude. And the dream stayed with me.

That night, with the company of a pint and my cat, Malkyn, I sat by my fire. The dream's import soon came clear. The woman in black was me. I was mourning Jankyn, my last, best, lustiest—and now dead husband. I'd known I missed him, but I'd buried my feelings in belligerence. My weavers did not love me for it, but their output soared and I took some real satisfaction in knowing the coffers were full. I looked forward to lechery's return.

But here I was, a year since his death, still alone, still longing for the old heat, our rages and our loving. Worse than a languishing lady in a honeyed romance. I was ashamed of myself and uneasy at the possibility that I might not be as tough as I'd thought.

I went back to the dream. It seemed to me that the other woman, the one in white, was another part of me. Perhaps in the wood I'd been trying to rescue myself. And perhaps the first part—the sunshine, the birds, the gentle horse—was a sign of hope, but I had to do something drastic to shake off my torpor.

It being April, the obvious choice was a pilgrimage. They ran regularly at that time of year between London and Canterbury. Though modest as pilgrimages go, the London-Canterbury plan would mean that I could leave immediately, and my weavers would not long be unsupervised. That someone bent on recovering the joys of lechery should decide to undertake a pilgrimage might seem strange to some, but not to me. Having been on more than a few in years past, I well knew that the motives and goals of pilgrims were many, but few were seriously religious, however holy the geographic destination.

꙳

London

I arrived at the Tabard Inn in Southwark last night in good time to reserve a horse for the morrow—a stylish ambler whose swaying gait would show me off to advantage. My chunky dapple I stabled in comfort at the hostelry so she'd be fresh for my return to Bath. I washed away the traces of my trip, then added some musky scent, some strategic colour. I brushed out my hair and donned my best outfit—new shoes, red stockings, a bright skirt tucked up to show off a bit of leg, a bodice cut low enough to be inviting but yet to encourage further exploration. I wanted my entry into the dining hall to create a stir, and so it did. All male heads swiveled, all male eyes were fixed as I sauntered by and appraised the assembled company.

They numbered nearly thirty and I was pleased to see that, with the exception of two nuns, all were men. A second perusal left me less sanguine. There were the usual ecclesiastical dregs—pardoner, friar, monk—variously vain, gluttonous and avaricious, and all repulsive. A gaggle of guildsmen, but some were from the cloth trade and I knew they would carry tales back to Bath. Besides, they looked as if they would do nothing unless they could do it together, which at present I was not interested in. A stuffy lawyer, a saintly parson and a portly poet—no, no. A drunken miller, a sour merchant, an ulcerous cook—no, no, no. My heart began to sink. Had I come all this way only to find such a motley crew?

But then I began to notice a few more attractive pilgrims. A much-travelled knight with his curly-haired son. A well-made, ruddy franklin. Better.... Yet I was sure that after all those crusades the knight would be a prig in bed and his son would be looking for some anemic young thing with blonde hair and one of those insufferably small waists. The franklin I could see was already casting fawning eyes on the knight, whose approval he yearned for—too much of a social climber.

The priest chaperoning the two nuns was a goodly specimen, burly and earthy, a worthy grapple. The challenge there would be to get him away from his lily-white charges—which might take more time than I had. A shipman with a piratical flair was tanned and muscled from his labours asea, and, if newly ashore, would be randy to boot. It was to his credit that his ship was called "Magdalene," after my favourite saint. A good prospect.

It was a while before dinner. We were being entertained by the usual assortment of musicians and tumblers, and the ale was flowing. There was time, I thought. I sat myself across from the shipman, and slid my leg over to his. After a few strokes under the table I had his attention, and I gave him a knowing look. A slow grin of comprehension creased his swarthy face. I took another swig and slowly licked my lips. He was hooked. I made as if to go to the privy and gave him a roll of the eyes. We met in the hall between the dining room and the kitchen, and slipped behind a stack of barrels. He was as ready as I was. Up with the skirt, down with the britches, and we were at it, our hands groping and our breath coming hard. The air was thick with garlic, ale, smoke and, best of all, a heady dose of that ultimate aphrodisiac, male sweat. He still tasted of the sea. He was upright as a mast and in like a divining rod. I was already on the way as he came aboard and that brought him right along so we finished together, panting and sweating, not taking time for a kiss.

In the dining room again before anyone noticed we were gone, I raised my glass to him. He'd served his purpose.

So I was back in action, and marvellously refreshed. My appetite was good, and so was the food. As the first course was in progress we were joined by our host, who introduced himself as Harry Bailly. He was a robust type, obviously starved for sex, and I was just the one to set matters right. Very good. He'd be a more complex case, though, than my shipman, so I bided my time.

After we finished our meal Harry proposed a plan. Each of us would tell a story on the way to Canterbury, and likewise on the way back to Southwark. He would travel with us to Canterbury as our guide. When we got back to the Tabard, the rest of us would buy dinner for the one who had told the best tale. As it promised to make for a lively trip, his plan met with general approval from the assembled company. In fact, we were pleased enough with Harry to insist that he be both our leader and the judge of the tales. Evidently few of us were intent on sackcloth and ashes.

As a lot we retired, satisfied in our respective ways, looking forward to an early start on the morrow.

Alone, I thought over the situation and had to admit that the outlook for the rest of my journey was bright. Most immediately I would have the luxury of my own room, since of course the nuns could not share with me—God forbid, they might be tainted by breathing the same air. Such privacy would have its obvious advantages.

Warmed by a glass of Harry's potent wine, I lay back to admire my red stockings. Tomorrow I must be sure to wear my new spurs. I doubted the ambler would need them, but I'd hope that some of my fellow travellers (who, as I mounted and hitched up my skirts, would already be eyeing my ankles) would find them piquant. Others would frown, but being villified for carnality by the pious was always gratifying.

In particular I was looking forward to scandalizing the prioress. 'Madame Eglentyne' was how she presented herself, clearly hoping for all the courtly, aristocratic aura such a name could conjure up. Admittedly she was pretty, though it was obvious to me that she was trying hard to look ten years younger than she was. A set of coral beads was wound fetchingly about her wrist, with a brooch engraved to read '*amor vincit omnia*' (such delicate ambiguity). Her wimple was arranged to show her smooth brow and cupid's-bow smile to full advantage.

What elegant table manners she had! How tender she looked as she fed her little lap dogs! Many of the men clearly thought she was just adorable. Needless to say she turned my stomach, not least because of her hypocrisy. I had watched her at dinner and she was obviously as interested in her power over these men as I was (travelling with her plain side-kick to make herself look better), but she hid behind a demure guise of chastity. I would have loved to tweak that darling retroussé nose.

I slept, and I dreamt. But alas, instead of riding the waves again with my salty pirate, I was beset by the 'unholy trinity,' as I was wont to call my first three husbands. It was a ghastly parade, each one older and scrawnier than the last. In life, I had eventually managed to get the upper hand over them, but in my dream they conspired to keep me down. They shook their bony fingers at me and reviled me for my infidelities. They locked me up. They took away my clothes and dressed me in an old smock. And worst of all, they exercized their conjugal rights.

I woke in a sweat, but could not banish the memories called up by the nightmare. With terrible clarity I recalled being sold off to the first one. I was twelve. Twelve, and barely a woman. But my loutish father, a miller with absurd social aspirations, saw the chance to better his name (and his purse), when a wealthy old merchant from the village asked for my hand—as if it were my hand he was after. That wedding night came back to me in every lurid detail. In his dotage my husband saw himself as the great lover. His own virility long gone, he stirred himself to semi-potency with spiced wine, and climbed atop me with reassurances that since we were married he had the church's blessing in doing anything he wanted. He'd had a long career as an amorous bachelor, keeping company with the tavern girls, and vainly tried to emulate their tricks. He failed, but his aphrodisiacs kept him going. I was raw and bruised, scratched by his sharp whiskers. His breath stank and the loose skin on his neck shook. He got playful. He called me his "own dear spouse." He sang me ballads from the brothel. He got the hiccups. His nose dripped. I felt sick. Finally towards dawn he fell asleep and I managed to extricate myself from the snoring pile of bones. I lay still, then, for a long time. I would not cry. I clenched my teeth. I tried to breathe, but oh, the stench. I hated him. I hated my father. And I hated my mother, because she had let him sell me, and because she had given me no inkling of the degradation I was to undergo. I made it to the privy, where the air was a little less foul, and sat down to think. There was no way out of this. It seemed that all I could look forward to was death, either my "dear spouse's" or my own. I devoutly hoped for his.

It was in that bleak dawn that, as an effort of will, I developed the first layer of my thick skin. I made up my mind that nothing again would ever hurt me as I had been hurt that night. And the 'marriage bed' never was that bad again. Revolting, yes. Boring, yes, oh yes. But never that bad.

I learned to appreciate the money and status that came with my new life; my husband liked to parade his trophy, and so dressed me well. The food was good. The house was roomy and well-furnished. I enjoyed looking down on my father. I liked having servants. And soon I developed some tricks of my own, another layer of skin. I wouldn't let him into bed until he had given me money—for a new hat, or shoes, or whatever trinket I had a yen for. After all, I thought, one commercial transaction deserved another. I also gradually began to notice that there were all manner of lovely young men in the village. They often soothed me with their lingering glances. Eventually my husband acquired a new apprentice—an ardent youth with beautiful blond hair. We grew to be very good friends, then successful co-conspirators. Through him I learned that the act of love could be sweet, and mutual. My husband had his suspicions, but I deflected them, which was not difficult since in his vanity he preferred to think that the new roses in my cheeks were due to his attentions.

And so it went. My husband took his pleasure, and I took mine, elsewhere. I suppose the physician who advised him so thoroughly on the subtleties of his aphrodisiacs might have warned him about the dangers of such energetic activity at his age. Fortunately, he didn't. In the third year of our marriage he succumbed, in the act. Oh happy coitus interruptus! I suppose he died happy. Perhaps by now, so many years later, I can even manage to hope he did. But words cannot express the relief I felt as I extricated myself for the last time from that wretched body.

My euphoria did not last long. My ownership reverted to my father. Some money had come with me on my husband's death (though most of course went to the nearest male relative). Evidently this turned me into a more valuable piece of goods. Before long I had another suitor, a little richer and a little older than my first. Of course there was the requisite period of mourning, which I savoured to the full. But all too soon my father was at work, brokering a new arrangement, and by the time I was sixteen I was introduced to my new fiancé.

The chill brought on by this recollection was happily interrupted by the sounds of a morning meal below. I barely paused to check my appearance in the glass—so glad was I to escape my memories—and descended, looking forward to some sweet bread and cider, a new day.

ॐ

Day One

It was a perfect April day, with a sweet westerly breeze wafting through the Tabard's open doors. After weeks of rain the skies had cleared to a crystal blue. Thoughts of the unholy trinity faded, and I began to look ahead to my plans for the day. Of course Harry was my target, but I was also looking forward to a country ride in the fresh sunshine, cheered by birdsong and new greenness.

As I looked about I noticed that we'd been joined by another pilgrim, a lanky, laconic clerk. He looked as though his main relationships in life had been with his books—he'd no doubt been upstairs with one last night as the rest of us were wining and dining below. I had a partiality for scholars because of Jankyn (after all, there was something to be said for a partner with whom one could match wits, and I well knew that a life of study did not preclude ardour abed). This one showed signs of intelligence and also an appealing diffidence. He moved with a grace of which he was obviously quite unaware, and his fine brown eyes watched the company with an ironic gaze. He struck me as a worthy long-term goal. I thought I would call him Troilus.

For the time being, though, I would keep my sights on Harry, and so went to my room to prepare for the day's ride. I did some work on my hair, added a little rouge to show off my cheekbones, some tint to bring out the green in my eyes and topped off yesterday's outfit with a grand new hat. I did not forget the spurs.

Our host gathered us together like a flock and led us out from the Tabard. Playing his bagpipes, the miller brought up the rear as we left the city, the spire of St. Paul's growing ever smaller in the distance. At the first watering place, two miles along the

Kent road, Harry asked us to draw straws as to who should tell the first tale, and it was no surprise that the knight won (as the noblest of our group, it was pretty clear that Harry wanted him to go first, and had fixed the draw.)

He assented with good cheer, and began his tale, which went something like this:

In long-ago and far-away Athens, the mighty duke Theseus is returning, victorious, from war. He passes a mourning group of women who beg for the burial of their dead. He magnanimously complies, restoring the bodies of their loved-ones to the women, and taking revenge on their slayer, Creon. In the ensuing pile of bodies he finds two wounded noble youths from the opposing side, whom he takes home with him and promptly locks in a tower for life. As it turns out they are cousins, Arcite and Palamon. They mourn their captivity for a while, but soon behold from the window of their prison a fair young woman, Emelye (Theseus' blond, virginal sister-in-law, fairer than the lily, and so forth), walking in the garden. Each instantly falls in love with her (she does not know they exist) and as instantly become one another's sworn enemy (each claiming to love her better). This goes on for what seems like years. Eventually, Arcite is freed at the request of an old friend of Theseus, on condition he never return. Palamon is left in the tower to mourn. Arcite is thus at liberty, but cannot see Emelye. Palamon is in prison, but can only watch her from the window. Each thinks his plight is more lamentable, ranting accordingly and at considerable length.

Arcite returns, disguised, to serve in Theseus' household and so be near Emelye. Palamon escapes. By chance, or perhaps by Fortune, who plays a big part in this story, they meet in the woods, and of course immediately want to kill each other. Arcite, as he has access to the court's supplies, is gentleman enough to offer to bring weapons and other necessities to the wood so that they can destroy one another properly. Next day as they are in the process of cutting each other to ribbons, Theseus happens along by chance (or this time perhaps by Destiny, God's agent).

Theseus decrees that in a year's time there should be a huge tournament, to decide which of the two shall win Emelye. (She's not consulted.) The cousins are allowed that time to amass their armies.

There are some great fighting scenes, but before that the young folk are seen at prayer. Arcite beseeches Mars for victory. Palamon begs Venus to grant him his lady. Meanwhile, Emelye prays to Diana. She does not want either one of them— she wants to remain chaste! At this point it seemed to me it would have made sense for P & A to shake hands and go off together, leaving Emelye alone with her precious virginity. However, the fight goes on, and there's also a furor in the heavens as Venus tries to get her own way—as usual she uses her charms and gets what she wants.

I couldn't decide whose side to be on since I was born under the influence of both Palamon's and Arcite's planets. I bear the seal of Venus as my birthmark, and from her I get my desire; yet my belligerence comes from Mars. I had to give Venus credit for her wiles. But it would have seemed fair for Arcite to get Emelye. He was the better fighter and that's what the tournament was supposed to be all about.

The tale turned out to have kind of a trick ending. Arcite, with the help of Mars, wins the tournament, but then Pluto (as a result of Venus' meddling) sends a thunderbolt from the below, which terrifies Arcite's horse. He is thrown, and fatally wounded. There is a grand funeral for Arcite, before which all three are reconciled. After an appropriate interval, Palamon and Emelye are united, and Theseus gives a wise speech about God's will, trying to make sense of what's happened.

To tell the truth, I'd expected the knight's tale to put me to sleep, but it wasn't half bad. Certainly it was far too long and showed I'd been right to suppose him a snob (rank was the measure of heroism) and a prig (the ideal woman prefers chastity). Still, his story had its strengths—I even felt a lump in my throat as poor Arcite lay on his death-bed and bade Palamon good-bye—

it was sad that the cousins who had once loved each other so well could only become friends again when one of them was dying such a useless death. To me, though, the young folk finally seemed a pretty dull lot. Palamon and Arcite took themselves too seriously. Emelye barely spoke a word and was so devoted to her virginity it was hard to see what she had to offer beyond her similarity to a lily. On the other hand Theseus, though he could be arrogant and obiously saw women merely as trophies, had his finer moments. And the battles were truly grand.

Now while listening to the knight I also kept an eye on my fellow-pilgrims and was intrigued to notice that Madame Eglentyne was his most attentive listener. As the tale went on, and she heard of the young men's passion and the duke's might and wisdom, she gradually moved her horse closer to his, her eyes exploring not only his earnest face, but also his manly physique. What could this mean? Was it possible that our demure prioress was actually feeling the stirrings of Venus? This bore watching.

When the knight's tale was ended there was much talk, especially amongst the gentlefolk, of how noble and memorable it was. Harry, clearly delighted his plan was working out so well, turned to the monk and invited him to go next. I suppose he thought he was going to go right down the social ladder, ending at the lowest rung. But human nature, in the brawny form of Robyn the miller, got in the way. He had put away his pipes as we were riding, and must have been hard at work on the ale—being now so drunk he could barely stay on his horse.

"By God's blood and bones," he cried, "I know a noble tale too. I'll match the knight's tale!"

Harry tried to dissuade him, but Robyn and his thick head would not be refused. He flared his huge black nostrils, thrust his unkempt red beard in Harry's face. He roared.

"Now, everybody, lishten to me! The firsht thing I have to shay is that I'm drunk. I can tell by the shound of my own voishe. Sho if I can't talk shtraight, blame it on the ale of Shouthwerk!"

In the manner of many a drunk, he found his own joke funnier than anyone else did, which did not bode well for his tale. In fact it was as vulgar and lewd as I might have expected, and hoped, but it was also surprisingly clever. Robyn somehow managed to keep track of all the story's strands and pull them together at the end—he must have had lots of practice telling and re-telling it at various stages of drunkenness. Luckily this was the first time for us. His tale went something like this:

There dwelt in Oxenford a rich and foolish old carpenter, John by name, who took in boarders. Just now his lodger is a clerk called Nicholas, a clever, comely young scholar, himself sweet as licorice. John is newly married, and his young wife Alison (I was amused that Robyn seemed to have named her after me) is lovely enough to charm the birds out of the trees—winsome, lively as a colt, slender as a weasel, her breath sweet as ale and honey. John is (as well he should be) jealous and tries to keep his wife locked up. But Nicholas is lusty, and so is Alison, and when the carpenter is away, their dalliance commences. Coy Alison is willing enough, though worried lest her husband suspect. Nicholas assures her that, as a clerk, he should certainly be able to fool a carpenter. Thus they make their plans, that they may lie together undisturbed and undetected.

The rest would seem obvious. But the situation is not so simple. Alison has another would-be lover, also a clerk (less clever than Nicholas, and more fastidious) named Absalon, vain as to his golden curls and his stylish dress, who frequents the taverns of the town with his guitar. He too seeks the love of Alison and often sings love-songs beneath her window, but such is her longing for Nicholas that she finds him a pest.

The lovers put their plan into action. They tell John that a flood—greater even than Noah's flood—has been foreseen by Nicholas and that if they are to survive they must hang tubs from the ceiling and each climb into one of them with sufficient provisions. Then, when the flood does come, they can cut the cords of their tubs and sail happily out into the garden. Gullible John, frantic for the safety of his sweet wife, weeps and wails.

"Go, dear spouse," cries Alison, and so he goes to get the tubs, fills them with food, builds the ladders. On the night of the supposed flood, they each climb to their hanging tubs and wait in silence. As anticipated, John is soon asleep and snoring. Nicholas and Alison creep down their ladders and into the carpenter's bed, to enjoy each other in comfort....

However, believing that John is away, Absalon hopes that tonight shall be the night he finally wins a kiss from his honeycomb, his fair bird, Alison. So beneath her window he sings, "I mourn as does the lamb after the teat."

Alison snaps that she loves another; "Go away! Let me sleep!" But Absalon will not leave without his kiss.

So out the window she puts her arse, which is promptly and ardently kissed by the squeamish clerk. "A woman has no beard!" he cries, distraught—and his hot love is quenched. "Tehee!" says she and slams the window shut.

Nicholas and Alison fall back into bed splitting their sides with laughter. But Absalon is not so easily dismissed. Rubbing his lips with dust, sand, straw—whatever he comes across—he goes to his friend the blacksmith and borrows a red hot plough-blade. Back he goes, and again begs for a kiss. This time Nicholas decides to get in on the act—he sticks out his arse and lets fly a thunderous fart. Absalon smites him with the red-hot iron. Nicholas, in agony, cries out "water! water!" John awakes, thinks the flood has come, cuts the cord to his tub, and crashes to the floor below. So John is cuckolded, Absalon has kissed his lady's arse, Nicholas is scalded in the bum—but Alison gets off scot-free. Perfect justice!

Most everyone seemed to be delighted by Robyn's show, though he was having a bit of fun at the knight's expense. Foolish John could be seen to stand for the wise Theseus, lusty Alison for the virginal Emelye, Nicholas and Absalon for Palamon and Arcite, and so on. But there was enough good feeling for the knight that not much was made of this and we stopped to let the horses have some water and take some lunch ourselves.

But speaking of the knight, where was he? And come to that, where was our lady Mme. E? Certainly not with us. Then I saw them coming up from behind, at some distance (the priest and second nun riding close by). Poor Eglentyne, I thought, in a brief moment of sisterly sympathy—how was she ever going to get anywhere with Braveheart (as I'd taken to calling the knight) if she was always to be followed by her shadows? Still, as the two approached, it looked to my tutored eye as if some progress had been made. They were deep in conversation. Her cheek was flushed and slightly turned from him—but not so far he was not able to see that lovely glow and know he had been the cause. Well, after all, I thought, perhaps love does conquer all!

୬

Eglentyne. I have often wondered why my parents bothered to give me that beautiful name, the name of a woman meant to be loved, if their plan was for me to end up in a Benedictine convent. They must have known that as the last of four daughters there would not be enough of a dowry for me to get a husband, that I'd have to sit by and watch while my sisters were wooed and married. Whatever their reason, I was hardly more than a child when I was packed off to the convent. I worked hard at my French lessons, developed ladylike manners, but I'll admit that as a novice I hoped I wouldn't have to stay. When at fifteen I took the veil and became officially 'dead to the world,' it was not because I wanted to but because there really was nowhere else for me to go.

I did try to be grateful, but the fact is I was bored and lonely. Prayer was supposed to be the most important part of our life in the nunnery. We had to get up in the middle of the night and traipse down to the chapel even in the dead of winter, but what I wanted was for someone to take me in his arms and tell me how beautiful I was. Most of the time the girls were forced to be silent, so we had to use sign language. It was hard to make friends (which I'm sure was St. Benedict's point) and certainly there was no way to speak about how I longed for a knight in armour to come along and rescue me. (Luckily I'd heard about Lancelot and Tristan from my real sisters before I was locked up.) Of course I knew I should 'tell all' to the priest in confession, but there was no way I'd chance that—I'd have to promise to give up my dreams and I knew I couldn't. I didn't want to. They were what kept me going, smiling sweetly so the priests and prioress would think I was divinely happy and leave me alone. One of the girls who talked back was beaten in front of the rest of us—that was enough to convince me to keep smiling.

Well, after a while the surface seemed to take over. I knew I was there somewhere underneath, but it got to be such a habit to be agreeable and follow the rules that it was hard even for me to make contact with myself. As the years went by I did get used to the convent—always kept up appearances and followed the rules. Then believe it or not, when our prioress died, it was decided that I should replace her. I guess they figured that a pretty prioress who could speak French and had good table manners would help attract the daughters of the upper classes. I thought, if only they knew what I really want. But then I thought, well maybe some of the other sisters want things that are much worse. After all, we are told that God is Love. Besides, I got my own apartment. I'll admit I liked that, and the power that came along with my new job. I could have pets, like the little dogs I have now, who keep me company and truly love me, and no one in the convent could stop me. When the bishop came by he pretended to be displeased, but when he saw me playing with the little creatures he obviously thought it was adorable and let me off. So I did what I liked, and I was admired, and I got used to being lonely.

Some more years went by, though, and my old longings came back, or came to the surface, I should say. I suppose they had been there all along. Sometimes I had dreams of a lover, or a child. I thought a lot about the Virgin Mother, who I liked more than God the Father (though of course I did not say so in confession), but at the same time I have to admit I felt a bit jealous of her. After all she had the best of both worlds—she had a husband, and a very devoted one at that, who did not mind her being pregnant by someone else. She was a virgin, which always served you well in the next life, but she also got to have a baby, and a pefect baby at that—more than any of the rest of us could hope for.

Last winter I was feeling lower than ever. Finally I decided that I would go on a pilgrimage, not for the sake of my soul, but just to get away from those walls. I knew I was not allowed to and that the bishop would disapprove, but I also knew I could bring him round, which I did. Of course he insisted that I take my priest and another nun along, which did not bother me since I was sure I could manage them. And so I found myself at the Tabard Inn, getting ready for a journey to the shrine of St. Thomas in Canterbury. He was supposed to help people when they were sick. Maybe a visit to him would make me feel better.

Last night we all had dinner together, though of course my chaperones insisted we sit at a separate table, I suppose so I would not be corrupted. Still, I got a look at the others. There was only one other woman, a loud show-off type who I was glad to see was older than me. Quite a few of the men were watching me so I made a point of putting on my best manners and letting them get a good view of my profile. But there was one who stood out right away—a real knight, who had just come back from a crusade. His tunic even showed the rust-marks of his armour. He was a head taller than any of the others, and had the most beautiful face—sad, wise, noble. I was even more drawn to him than I had been to the knights in my dreams. It felt lovely, and a little scary. I thought I had at least that much coming to me after all my years of being dutiful. I was too excited to sleep much.

Today *he* was the first to tell a tale, and it was everything I would have expected from him. It was about the undying adoration of two young knights for a beautiful young woman named Emelye—who I have to say reminded me a bit of myself. They had only to see her from afar to fall totally in love with her. After that nothing else mattered to them. They had been best friends but now became sworn enemies. Finally in the end one of them was killed in a cruel accident, so the other, the one who had prayed to Venus, got to marry Emelye. Together they were rich and lived happily ever after. Emelye loved him tenderly and he served her so faithfully that there was never a cross word between them. It was even better than the stories of Lancelot and Tristan, who never did get to marry their ladies.

I watched the knight as he was telling his story and his face became even more beautiful. He seemed to feel the suffering of the young knights so keenly. I could tell he was a true gentleman, and would be a wonderful lover himself, if only he had the right lady.

Then I discovered what true kindness and nobility really are. After the knight had finished, the miller started off on a drunken tale that was obviously going to be one bit of smut after another. And there I was caught in the middle of the group. I was blushing and felt horribly embarassed but did not know how to get away. I knew I ought to have stayed a little closer to my priest. Suddenly the knight moved his horse over to mine, took hold of my bridle and led me back where we could not hear. I was so overcome I couldn't say anything for a while, not even thank you, but he just quietly rode along beside me and let me take my time. Finally we talked a bit and I said how fine his story was, how I was sorry that one knight had had to die, but how I was glad that Palamon and Emelye could love each other so well.

He said he was "honoured that someone whose esteem he valued had approved his tale." Those were his exact words! He told me his name was Richard—just like our king!—and asked me mine. Then he led me back to my priest—I suppose he realized he shouldn't keep me to himself for too long—and said he hoped we could talk again during the journey. Oh Richard, Sir Richard! I can hardly wait!

༄

As we set out after lunch it soon became clear that Oswald the reeve had been building up a real head of steam. It transpired that he too is a carpenter and thought the miller was insulting him personally with his tale of the cuckolded John. Considering how angry he was there was no chance of his being turned away, any more than there had been with Robyn this morning.

Oswald's tale featured Symkyn, a social-climbing miller (famous for cheating his clients), his wife and daughter (for whom he seeks an upper-crust marriage), and two young clerks from Cambridge. The clerks bring their grain to the mill intending to outsmart the miller. He sees what they are up to and tricks them instead. It being late, they are forced to stay overnight and manage to turn the tables once again, ending up in bed with the wife and daughter (one apiece), while Symkyn snores and farts alone. When he finally awakes and realizes (dimly) what's been going on there is a huge fight in the pitch-black; the clerks beat him soundly and ride off with their flour.

The way Oswald told his story, the miller deserved eveything he got, but Robyn was drunk enough to completely miss the insult. The cook, only slightly more sober than Robyn (I was glad he wasn't doing our cooking), found the tale of the miller's trouncing hilarious and launched into his own. He didn't get far (a blessing, considering how witless he was) because the April rains had left the roads so swampy that it was all we could do to struggle through the mud towards Dartford.

Oswald's greedy, pretentious Symkyn had reminded me of my own father and thoughts of him kept me preoccupied for a while. Once again I recalled my first marriage and my anger at having been disposed of in that way. I remembered coming home after number one's death and how eager my father had been to sell me off again, paying no heed to my pleas for a respite. Being a little older and considerably wiser about the realities of marriage, I was more aware of the way he treated my mother—insulting her, beating her, flaunting his infidelities. I thought she'd have hated him as much as I did. But the pathetic creature worshipped him. She'd cringe and apologize, and promise to do better. I tried to talk to her—to say he was acting like a brute—but she would hear none of it. He was God's gift to her and if she failed to please him, it only showed her own unworthiness—she'd have to try harder, or at least bear her punishment meekly.

So I was passed on to my new owner, number two. There was not much to distinguish him from his predecessor except that he was less given to aphrodisiacs and more prone to the use of force. He and my father agreed that this was likely the best way to manage me since I showed signs of being headstrong. My father told him confidentially that he had used the birch to great effect in his own situation, bringing about a most pleasing sub-servience in my mother.

Being beaten when I was not properly obedient vied with my first wedding night as the most unpleasant experience of my life, but soon led me to expand my survival strategies. Playing on my new spouse's pre-eminent vanity, I tried accusing him of infi-delity. This pleased him because he thought I believed him virile enough to be carrying on elsewhere, and because he took my accusation as a sign that I cared. Meanwhile I was casting my eye about for any comely young man in the neighbourhood who would enjoy a walk in the fields. This worked out well enough. Since he took it to mean he was potent and adored, he put up with my scolding and I was glad of my refreshments amongst the hay. Once again, I did not mind being rich, and having servants, and looking down on my father. I was getting by—but still, I thought, as between my mother and myself, what a way to live. I certainly could not believe that, if there was a God, this was what he intended for women.

With a minimum of slipping and sliding I managed to sidle my ambler over to Harry as we neared Dartford. I told him my name, and said I just wanted to thank him for agreeing to be our host on the way to Canterbury. Then I asked him what he thought of the knight's tale.

"It was truly grand," he said. "What a fine fellow that knight is! His nobility shines through in every word he speaks."

"Yes," I agreed. "I liked Theseus best of all. he was so masterful. You know, in some ways he reminds me of you." Harry looked surprised, and asked why.

"Well, he had to deal with so many difficult things—those grieving women, the young knights trying to kill each other, and so on. You have to do the same with us pilgrims, trying to keep us, well, orderly. It was right for the knight to go first and I know that was your doing. Then when Robyn and Oswald got troublesome you handled them just as Theseus would have. Really, masterful's the only word for it. I just think we're so lucky to have you." Harry glowed.

"Why, Alison—thank you. I suppose because I see so much of that sort of thing at the Tabard—too much drink, you know, and then people wanting to get back at each other—it's hard to know when to step in, but you're right, it's easy for bad feelings to break out and once that happens, well, then getting the good feeling back is very hard."

"Harry, you're a fine man," I said, and I meant it. "I wish there were more like you."

And so we continued until our inn came into view.

After the long day and that last bit of struggling through the mud everyone seemed both hungry and tired. We ate our dinner, which was tasty enough, and drank our share of wine and ale sitting around a lovely big fire. Troilus was not in evidence. I supposed he was upstairs with his book again. I went up to my little room—Mme. E. and her shadow got the best quarters, of course—the innkeeper had fallen all over himself to please her—but I was glad enough to be alone. I'd made some progress with Harry and the fact was I actually did like him. I'd got a fair view of his barrel chest as we were talking and knew he would be both comfortable, and comforting, in bed.

Such thoughts took me back to Jankyn, not too surprisingly—missing him had been why I'd come on this journey in the first place. I remembered the funeral of number four. I'd put on a show of weeping but he had turned out to be a nasty bit of work, cheating on me so's everyone could see and taunting me for being too old to keep his interest. I certainly wasn't sorry to see him go. From behind my handkerchief I was keeping a close eye on the legs of the young clerk Jankyn, who was just ahead of me in the procession to the churchyard. I think I fell for him on the spot and it didn't take long for me to let him know. In fact, we were married by month's end. We were great in bed, but well-matched in other ways too, as to humour and wit. Of course he had the upper hand when it came to learning, but I was sharp and picked things up quick as could be. We laughed and we made love and we fought—didn't we fight!—especially in the beginning.

As a clerk Jankyn had of course been schooled in woman-hating and loved to tease me by reading aloud about the frailties of the female sex—how Eve was responsible for the fall of man, how such great men as Samson were ruined by their women, how various wives had slain their unsuspecting husbands, how impossible it was for a woman to be both fair and chaste.

I tried not to let him get to me (not wanting to give him the satisfaction), but inside I was smouldering. One night he finally went a little too far. I grabbed his book, ripped out a fistful of pages, and pushed him backwards into the fire. Wild as a lion he leapt up and knocked me to the floor.

I moaned. "Oh, you've murdered me!" Then I added, pathetically, "but ... before I die ... let me kiss you one more time." Beside himself with grief, he knelt down for my kiss. I hit him full in the face, crying that now I was avenged and could die in peace.

Dying was not what I had in mind, of course. I struggled up and we went at it hammer and tongs, panting and hot with rage as we grabbed and clawed and tore at each others' clothes. But it wasn't long before we began to see the humour of the situation; despite ourselves we started to laugh and the more we laughed the sillier we seemed. We collapsed in front of the fire and pulled off what was left of our clothes. The flush of our rage and our struggle stayed with us and we made beautiful hot love, biting, scratching and laughing all the while.

Later we sat and talked, sharing a bottle of wine we'd warmed in the embers of the fire. What he offered was to stop his teasing and "put the bridle in my hand." I agreed, on condition that he burn his wretched book. He—or rather we—did, and by its flickering light we lay back to go at it one more sweet time.

჻

Eglentyne. My roomate had said her prayers and was deep in a pure virginal sleep. She was probably dreaming about Cecilia, her favourite saint, after whom she'd been named. She'd already told me that when it came her turn to tell a tale it would be about her heroic martyrdom. St. Cecilia's story had always been hard for me to believe. She was a Roman maiden who was married to a noble youth named Valerian. But she was such a devout Christian that she prayed she would be allowed to remain a virgin. She even wore a hair shirt under her golden wedding dress! On her wedding night she told her husband that there was an angel guarding her and that if he touched her he would be slain. Valerian was a bit supicious—who could blame him?—but when he saw the angel he was converted. Then another angel appeared in their bedroom and gave them each a crown of lilies, meaning that they were going to live a pure life together—both as virgins! Cecilia went on to convert masses of pagans and was very brave when she was finally killed by the wicked Romans, but I could never get over the fact that she had given up a perfectly good chance to be happily—I mean *really* happily—married to such a good-looking, well-off husband. Of course I never told anyone, but if I'd been in her shoes I certainly wouldn't have turned him down.

Needless to say I couldn't sleep for thinking about *him.* I sat by the window listening to the rain. I played with my little hounds (who I'd secretly named Tristan and Isolde) and fed them some bits of meat and bread I'd brought from dinner. They curled up on their little silk cushions and soon were asleep. I wondered if they were dreaming about running away together. I'd taken off my wimple and stroked my curls as I looked in my little mirror. Oh, they were pretty. Yes, I knew I wasn't supposed to let my hair grow long—and I certainly wasn't supposed to have a mirror (which I had begged from my big sister on one of her visits). Well. I didn't care. I did my job. I kept smiling. What more could they ask?

I was worried about what my tale should be. I wished I could just talk to Richard alone. But I also thought I had to go before the other women—especially that horrid common one—if I wanted to show them all that I was their superior and Richard's equal. After all, *he* had been the first of the men to go.

I finally did go to sleep, trying to decide on a story that would be proper for a prioress, but would also show *him* how tender and loving I really was deep down inside.

ॐ

I was in a sort of trance, remembering Jankyn, when I heard someone knocking at my door. I stayed quiet.

"Alison, it's me, Len. You know, Leonard, the shipman." So that was his name. He was the last person I wanted to see. Luckily I had bolted the door. I started to make a quiet snoring noise so he'd think I was asleep. He knocked again.

"Let me in, Alison. Please. I need to see you." I snored a little louder. He knocked a few more times and tried the door. Finally I heard him shuffle away down the hall. I heaved a sigh of relief and hoped he got the message. He could really get in the way as I tried to close with Harry, not to mention Troilus.

A storm had blown up outside, wind crying and rain pelting against the window-panes. I felt empty and terribly alone as I moved under the covers. I knew Jankyn would not come to me in my dream. I could be consoled by thinking about our times together, but he was gone. I had to accept that.

When I finally did sleep the terrible dream of the baby came back. It was winter. He was at the edge of a deep pit, crying, and I was trying to run towards him. The ground was icy and I slipped as I ran, my feet catching in the frozen roots. I was reaching out, calling his name, but I couldn't seem to get any closer. He tottered, in his sweet babylike way, and then he fell. I got to the edge of the pit. It was too dark to see but I could still hear him crying. I tried to grope my way down to get to him but there was nothing to hold onto, and then the crying stopped, and I knew he was dead. I lay on the hard ground, feeling as if my heart had been torn out, my tears freezing as they ran down my temples and into my hair, the sleet forming a shroud of ice. I wanted to lie there until I was so cold I could stop feeling. But the pain went on and on.

Day Two

I woke up the next morning feeling terrible. It had been years since I'd had that dream. I'd hoped it was gone for good. First the unholy trinity and now this. I wondered what would be next. Was it something about being on a pilgrimage that was stirring all this up? I pulled on my clothes and went downsstairs in a foul mood.

Who should I run into first but Len, greeting me with a woeful hound-dog look. I shot him a look of pure poison and hoped that would do to keep him at a distance. Next I saw darling Mme. E. and her shadow, keeping to themselves by the window. As usual E. was coyly showing off her neat manners and making herself even more adorable by daintily feeding tidbits to her little canine pests. Her male audience (of which she pretended to be quite unaware) was utterly charmed. It was enough to put me off my feed. I stuffed some bread in my pocket for later and stomped outside. The rain had passed and it looked to be a fine day. The inn was close by the Thames and I breathed in the strong smell of brine and mud and fishy seaweed that comes with a low tide. It was a big improvement.

Soon enough we set off towards Rochester, our horses splashing through the puddles. The sun came out in earnest and I ate some of my bread, which turned out to be sweet and fresh, and I started to feel better.

Ever the host, Harry began to fidget. It seemed he had not let go of his hierarchy plan, because this time he approached the lawyer and asked him for a tale. I wished Harry had not been so traditional. It was obvious before this man even opened his mouth that he was a pompous ass. But of course he was pleased to accept the offer, obviously believing it to be his due.

My fears were confirmed before he even started his story. He led off with an attack on poverty (à propos of what?), presenting the poor as a shameful lot—forever stealing, begging or borrowing. "Better to be dead than poor," he said solemnly. "Your own neighbours, your brother and your friends will all hate you." According to him, if people were poor it was their own fault, they had no one to blame but themselves. On the other hand (of course) rich merchants were greatly to be admired. I'd heard that when Wat Tyler and his peasant troops, armed with their cudgels and pitchforks, stormed London a few years back, the first people they went for were the lawyers. Listening to this one I could certainly see why. I wished they'd managed to catch him and put his head on the end of a pike along with all the others.

This wish grew stronger as he launched into his story. It was about one of those unbearable women who live to suffer, who glory in their humilation, and who are rewarded in the end for all their misery.

Constance is a beautiful Christian maiden, daughter of the emperor, who lives in Rome. Word of her extraordinary virtue reaches the ears of the Syrian sultan, who falls in love with her reputation, and vows to convert to Christianity if her father will agree to their marriage. He does. Constance is of course not consulted and she is shipped off in tears to Syria. Now this king has a spiteful, envious mother who is opposed to the union. She devises a plan which involves dismembering all the Syrians who have converted, including her son (!), and has Constance put to sea again.

She drifts for years, protected and fed miraculously by God. Eventually she washes up on the shores of Northumberland where, after being cared for by a good constable and his wife, she finds herself having to repel the advances of a wicked, lecherous knight. Spurned, he kills the constable's wife and tries to blame it on Constance. But in court he is struck down by the hand of God, and so Constance's innocence is proven. The English king, his heart melted by her helplessness, converts, executes the false knight and weds her. "Thus," noted the lawyer, "has Christ made Constance a queen."

Now this king coincidentally also has a spiteful, envious mother, who contrives to separate the newlyweds by means of forged letters and scurrilous lies—but a child has already been conceived. ("Though wives are such holy things, they must patiently put up with such demands as are pleasing to those who have married them.") Once more Constance is set adrift, this time with her little son. They wash ashore in an unknown land, where a wicked, lecherous apostate tries to have his will with her—but God pushes him overboard and he is drowned. "Oh, foul sin of lechery, such is thy end!"

Meanwhile, her father, having heard of what happened in Syria, sends troops to slaughter the remaining Syrians. On the way home they run into Constance who is drifting around the Mediterranean. Back at Rome her identity eventually becomes known and she is reunited with her Northumbrian king who, (remorseful for having killed his treacherous mother), has come to Rome as a penitent. After a year her husband dies and Constance lives happily ever after with her father.

Growing up I'd heard plenty of stories of women just like Constance and I knew what they were all about. We girls were supposed to try to be like them. Follow orders. Keep your mouth shut. Accept suffering. Passivity is the ultimate female virtue. If you are truly submissive you will be rewarded by God. Powerful women are always corrupt and insanely jealous of beautiful, younger women.

And of course, almost incidentally, all pagans are evil and deserve to die. To the lawyer there was no irony in having the newly-Christian king slay the knight and his own mother, or in having the emperor arrange for the slaughter of the Syrians. Well, I could certainly understand revenge—I'd inflicted plenty of it on the holy trinity—and forgiveness was not an art I'd ever tried to cultivate. I still hated my father, though he'd been dead for years.

But killing in the name of Christ struck me as going a bit too far.

When the lawyer had ended with a smug prayer, Harry turned to the parson (as he had to the monk yesterday) and asked him for a tale. But once again his plan was disrupted, this time by my tipsy friend Len, who wanted no philosophical sermon; he'd tell a merry tale that would wake us up. I knew right off that his would be a story about a wife cheating on her husband—I suppose he wanted to show how racy he could be—but I wanted to snub him and reined in my horse until I was out of earshot. I was pleased to find Harry at the back of the company. His manly nose was out of joint and he, too, wanted to show his disdain for the unruly shipman's offering. I was even more pleased to see the broad smile with which he greeted me.

"Well, Alison, I'm glad to see you, but you do not look pleased."

"Oh, Harry, I'm more than glad to ride with you. It was the shipman's rudeness to you that upset me, that and the endless story of that windbag lawyer."

Harry, taken aback, asked what it was about the tale of Constance that I hadn't liked.

"She seemed to me," he added, "such a delicate creature who suffered so much misfortune through no fault of her own." I didn't quite know where to start. If Constance was really Harry's ideal I had a rough row to hoe. But I gave it a try.

"Harry, I have to be honest with you. There aren't many people I trust, but I feel as if I can confide in you."

He liked that. I went on.

"The thing about Constance that I couldn't stand was that she had no will of her own. She was pushed and pulled around like a puppet by everyone. There wasn't any *heat* to her. It's easy to be pure," I added, "if all you want is to live happily ever after with your father. The only thing she was good at was drifting."

Harry mused. "I suppose I can see your point," he said generously, though obviously not convinced. "But there are some men who have had too great a dose of the opposite." At first I thought uncomfortably that Harry had somehow heard of my carryings on, but then I realized he must be talking about himself.

"Harry," I said, knowing that I was moving away from our topic, "you probably wouldn't be aware of this, but there are some husbands who use their wives very badly, beating them, keeping them locked up, and so on. I know that God wants us to obey him, but I can't believe the rest of it—that wives are likewise supposed to worship and obey their husbands no matter how they are treated."

I hesitated. "To tell the truth, Harry, I don't believe that men are superior to women. Sometimes when they have the power they abuse it terribly." Harry looked shocked.

"Alison," he said with feeling, "are you, by chance, speaking of your own experience?" Now it was my turn to be taken aback. I wasn't used to such sensitivity in men.

"Harry," I finally said, "I think we've both been through some hard times. Awhile back, I had the same feeling, that you were talking about yourself." He started, and I knew I'd been right. "I wonder if we could spend some time together, maybe tonight when we get to Ospringe, and talk about this some more. I know it would make me feel better." He was too much of a gentleman to refuse, but from the look in his eyes I could tell he was glad to be able to say yes.

Rochester was coming up, and it would be time to change horses and take some food and drink at the local alehouse. I put my hand on his arm. "Thank you," I said, and gave him a heart-felt look Mme. E would have died for.

⁓

Eglentyne. The sun shone brightly this morning and all the world seemed fresh and new from last night's rain. How I wished I could wear something more springlike than my wimple and habit. I looked as if I were in mourning! Still I washed carefully and pinched some colour into my cheeks, and went down with sister Cecilia, Tristan and Isolde scampering ahead. The inn-keeper seemed quite taken with me. Last night he gave us the best guest room, which had a beautiful oriel window, woolen rugs, and down-filled bedding. This morning he put us in the sun-filled bay window and brought us sweet bread and bits of bacon done to a turn. He also put a little bowl filled with primroses, which I suppose he had just gathered, by my place. I repaid him with my sweetest smile. He flushed, and bowed, and seemed content. Cecilia would have been happier with stale bread and cold water. It would have suited her nature, but she ate a bit. For myself, I enjoyed the innkeeper's offerings, though the bacon was a bit common. Thanks to Cecilia's self-denial, there was plenty left over for Tristan and Isolde, who begged very prettily for their treats.

I did not look around but I thought I could feel Richard's presence in the room. How I wanted him to love me! I'd always taken it for granted that men would find me pretty, and of course I liked it, but this was different. None of the others had ever meant anything to me. One was the same as the next. But now I wanted Richard himself to love me. Not only that, I felt a strange fluttering in my heart for him. Well, this was certainly going to be something *not* to mention in confession!

The lawyer started off the day with the tale of Constance, a Christian maiden who was both brave and beautiful. A pagan sultan from a far-off land loved her so much that he converted and begged her father the emperor for her hand. But his wicked mother was jealous and arranged for him and his friends to be killed. Constance was set to sea and though she drifted for years she never lost her faith and God watched over her. Next time she landed in England. The king there fell in love with her too, and so she became a queen. But his mother was also jealous and had her sent off again in her boat, this time with her baby boy. There were more adventures but Constance was always taken care of by God. Finally she was reunited with her husband—who had never stopped loving her—and later her son was crowned emperor.

The tale was a good example of how much God wants us to be patient no matter what. Of course I hadn't had any adventures (at least until I came on this pilgrimage) but I knew I'd been *very* patient during my many years in the convent and I certainly hoped God had noticed. The other thing I liked about the story was that it showed how women can be virtuous without having to be shut up in a convent or be baby-sat by chaperones. Constance was just as good after she got married and had a baby as she had been before!

Richard was riding not far from me during the lawyer's tale and I had a chance to smile at him a few times. He nodded back, very gravely. He is so serious. I think he must have had some sadness in his life, but he has his son with him so he must have been married sometime (maybe he still is! I hope not, though I suppose that means I also have to hope his wife is dead!). The next tale was by the shipman, a coarse fellow, also a bit drunk but not as bad as the miller yesterday. I knew his tale would be one I shouldn't hear but I didn't want to seem too forward by expecting Richard to protect me again, so I moved over to Cecilia and my priest. That would show him that I had a proper sense of decorum. I did overhear that the person the woman in the tale was carrying on with was a *monk*, so it was good that I missed the rest, not that I wasn't a little curious!

I stayed with my group when we stopped for lunch and got new horses. Mine was a delicate chestnut mare with a glossy mane who looked quite elegant under my side-saddle. Riding her made me feel like a lady in a courtly romance. The host turned to me and graciously said he hoped I would not be offended if he asked me to tell the next story. I suppose he wanted something to raise the tone after the shipman's tale, and also to show proper respect to my rank.

Luckily I had thought about what sort of tale I should tell (I'd decided to tell one based on some sermons I'd heard in the convent), so I said I was was glad to oblige. But first I offered a prayer to the Virgin Mary and begged her to guide me as I told my tale.

In far-away Asia lives a widow and her little son. In the midst of their city is a quarter inhabited by wicked Jews who carry on all sorts of hateful practices. Through this quarter runs a street which many a Christian is forced to use. The child must pass along it to get to his school at the other end. Now this boy, though so young, has a special love for the Virgin and he prays to her whenever he sees her image. One day he hears the other students singing a beautiful song, "Alma redemptoris mater," but he does not know Latin, so he cannot understand it. He asks an older school-mate, who explains that it is a hymn to the blessed mother of our saviour. The little boy vows to learn it by heart and studies so well that soon he can sing it word for word and note for note. Twice each day he sings the hymn, once on the way to school and once on the way home.

But Satan stirs the Jews to anger, saying how could they abide this insult? So they conspire to bring about the child's death and hire a murderer who cuts his throat and throws his body in the privy.

Meanwhile, when the boy does not come home, his mother is wild with dread and searches everywhere for him, always praying to the Virgin. Finally she learns that the last place he'd been seen was in the Jews' quarter, so there she goes to seek him, amongst those cursed people, who ever answer "nay" when she asks if they'd seen her child. But Jesus inspires her to cry out for him, whereupon, even as he lies in the privy with his throat cut, he begins to sing "O Alma redemptoris mater." The Christian folk come to marvel and the magistrate is sent for. The Jews are bound and the little boy, still singing, is carried to the abbey. Overcome with grief, his mother lies beside his bier. The magistrate decrees that every Jew who had knowledge of this crime shall be drawn by horses, and hanged.

After the funeral mass the child still sings and the abbott begs him to tell how this was possible. "My throat is cut to the neckbone," he replies, "but Jesus wills that for the sake of his dear mother I shall still be able to sing her praise." He goes on to explain that the Virgin had placed a magical grain upon his tongue that would allow him to keep on singing. "My little child," she'd said, "I will fetch you when the grain is taken from your tongue. Don't be afraid, I will not forsake you." So the holy monk takes the grain away and the child gives up the ghost. Everyone falls to the ground, weeping and praising Christ's mother; and then they enclose his sweet little body in a marble tomb, where it still lies. God grant that we may meet with him in heaven. Amen.

I was so overcome by sorrow for the boy's mother and by reverence for the Virgin who could work so great a miracle, that my eyes filled with tears and I could hardly get through the last prayer. The others were quiet for a time, until the host began to joke and turned to ask another pilgrim for a tale. I could not bear this, and pulled my horse aside where I rode alone for a bit. Then I knew, even before I saw him, that Richard had moved to my side.

"Eglentyne," he said. I felt a thrill. "I see you are moved by the little child's death, and by his mother's pain." He was silent for a time, but finally went on. "I would like to talk with you about your tale, but I fear you are still too grieved. Could I beg of you the favour of your company, perhaps this evening, after we have dined?" I was pleased by his being so gentle, and a-tremble at his request. Of course I said yes.

࿆

We had a good feed at the alehouse, which we needed, as we had quite a ways to go to Ospringe and its inn that night. Back on the road, I saw Mme. E. and her silly side-saddle, looking pleased as could be on her pretty new horse. I had a sinking feeling Harry was going to ask her to tell the next tale—he was too much of a traditionalist not to—and sure enough he did. Of course she sweetly agreed and launched into a prayer to the Virgin. That was my cue to exit.

I turned down to a wooded footpath that ran along side the Canterbury road. I could still see the group up ahead, but I was hidden by undergrowth and found a welcome stillness as I rode along on my own, still thinking about my talk with Harry and the story of Constance. I had been honest with him, but honesty is almost always partial. There was a lot I had *not* told him—my hearing such stories when I was a girl, my doubts about slaughtering pagans in the name of God. But also I hadn't told him about my mother. I knew that one of the reasons Constance and her type irked me was because my mother spent her life trying to be like them. She accepted every kind of abuse from my father. She was lonely and thought she was a failure. Her husband turned out not to love her after all, her reward was to be treated like a scullery maid, not a queen. And her son certainly didn't end up being crowned emperor. One night when my father was trying out new ways to torment her he held my little brother over the well and threatened to drop him in. Oh, he didn't mean to, but he was drunk, and slipped, and down went the baby. With a little moan my mother ran to the well and tried to throw herself in after him. My father held her back, laughing, enjoying the tussle—saying to himself "isn't this the hussy?" and to her "no matter, I can get another on you," he hauled her back into the house.

Some villagers finally managed to fish the baby out, but he was never quite right after that. When she produced another daughter, it was her fault of course—it hardly mattered, anyhow, since the poor thing only lasted a few days.

That's just one story. Many a time he'd bring women home, make her serve the two of them, then sit and wait while they went at it upstairs, thumping and carrying on so's there'd be no doubt as to what was happening. Afterwards he'd say to her, "What's wrong with you that you can't do it like that? Can you blame me for going with other women?"

And the worst of it all was she'd say, "No, Thomas, I don't blame you."

At long last she was released. One bright fall day my father was down at the mill, trying to repair the big wheel. Unsteadied by his mid-day tippling, he somehow managed to be pulled down and crushed beneath it as it began to turn. When I heard the news I was overjoyed, on my own account, and on hers. I hurried over to celebrate with her only to find her in tears, utterly devastated. She knelt beside his battered corpse, stroking his face and hair, clutching his hand in hers. "Oh Thomas—dear husband," she wept, "don't leave me! I know I haven't deserved you. Please come back. I promise I'll do better."

Some other women had come to help her lay him out but she wouldn't let them near him. All that night she crouched sobbing on the stone floor beside him, berating herself for her various failures. God had taken him because she hadn't been worthy of him and so on. Finally at dawn we had to drag her away.

The midwife, who had come in with the others and knew about herbs, got her to drink a tea of nettle and camomile, and at last she slept. But when she awoke, and remembered, she fell into a state of utter despair. She would not eat, she hardly slept. She'd been a strong woman—thanks to all the work she'd done waiting on him and scrubbing his floors—but she began to waste away. The priest used to visit, warning her about the sin of wanhope, about the blasphemy of not accepting God's will. This didn't help at all. She only wept some more and said he was right, she was worthless, she'd be better off dead.

At last I came up with a plan. The year before I had been relieved of the presence of husband number two. His passing had not only left me free (a state I planned to make the most of) but also with a bit of money. I proposed to my mother that we should take a pilgrimage together. Of course she refused. The only place she wanted to go, she said, was to the churchyard to join her Thomas. But I craftily pointed out to her that if she hoped to be with him in the next world she'd better set about doing some serious penance for her failures in this one. A modest pilgrimage, to Canterbury or even to Compostella, would not do. It had to be Jerusalem, if she wanted to convince God she was really sorry. And, I reminded her, dear Thomas would be looking down from above, and would surely be touched by this proof of her devotion. So I brought her round to the idea.

We packed our trunks and got ready for the journey. I hoped it would cure her melancholy, but was also looking forward to it myself. I was more than ready for some new horizons. Jerusalem had long ago ceased being a battleground between Christian and pagan, having been re-taken by the Turks. The Christians who stayed were merchants who lived peaceably with their heathen neighbours and made a tidy profit on the tourist trade. Twice a year, at Easter and Christmas, pilgrims came from far and wide to do penance, or for a change of pace, a holiday.

After crossing the channel we travelled overland through Burgundy and Lombardy to Venice. From there we sailed to Jerusalem. It was no hardship to leave the December chill behind. Each day seemed a little warmer. England had its charms, but I'd never imagined anything like the rich, sun-baked colours of the earth as we moved south, the vineyards with their tangled arbours, the gnarled rows of olive trees. And Venice was like a fairy city. Asail on the Mediterranean, the wind was warm as high summer, the water clear blue and golden, like day to the night of the channel's grey, angry waves. I'd spent a lot of time being angry at God for the way my life, and my mother's, had turned out, but I began to feel something like wonder at this new beauty. Perhaps, after all, a kindly God had made the creation in his own image and its ugliness was just the work of men.

But my mother refused to be moved. She wept and she prayed, and she wept some more. She'd heard somewhere about sackcloth and ashes and self-flagellation. Before we left she'd filled a little pouch with some ashes from the hearth and each morning of our trip she rubbed streaks of it on her cheeks. She kept asking where the flagellants were—she wanted to join them. I started to lose patience with her, but she'd managed to find some other pilgrims who were just as intent upon their misery as she was, so she hardly noticed.

We went by donkey from Jaffa to Jerusalem, where I left her sighing and moaning with her new friends. I went off to see the sights—the Mount of Olives, the mosques, the strange vaulted streets of the city, the Saracen bazaar. I bought a souvenir. It was supposed to be a piece of the stone from the sepulchre, though I had my doubts, and took it back to my mother. She almost smiled and said she'd keep it with her always as a reminder of her unworthiness. Not exactly what I'd had in mind.

On the way back she said she'd learned from one of her friends that it was possible for widows to take the veil, though of course they wouldn't be quite as holy as the real virgins. She'd decided that this was how she wanted to end her days. At one point I'd hoped she might be able to begin a new life in the real world—she was hardly forty—but by now I'd given up. So the mill was sold. Most of the money was put aside for the care of my poor brother, who could not look after himself. Some went to make up a dowry that would allow my mother to enter a convent not far from our village. There wasn't much left for me. I did visit her a few times, but she said the nuns were told they should forget their bonds with this world. She would pray for me, but I'd better not come back. So there she stays. I can't imagine she's happy, but I hope she's at least less miserable.

The glow I'd felt sailing to Jerusalem evaporated. I felt more bitter towards God than ever. I was alone in the world. No one was going to take care of me but myself. I suppose that's what led me to the third person of the unholy trinity, though looking back it's hard to believe I could ever have freely made such a choice. But being married to a rich old fool was the only life I knew. And survival was the issue, not 'happiness' (whatever that was). The money I had wouldn't keep me for long, but as a dowry it was an attraction of sorts. I was young for a widow, and handsome. In short, I was a good bargain, and so I set about the business of selling myself to the best customer.

Well, after husbands one and two there was not much that could hurt or surprise me. Number three was a cloth-maker whose business was in St. Michael's parish, just north of Bath. I loved being so near the city, its noisy crowds, its colours and smells—I was more than glad to trade the gillyflowers' fragrance for the stench of old fish and stale beer. And the taverns, the markets, the travelling actors! I'd been to Jerusalem, but I'd never seen a play! They were a big improvement on the lives (and deaths) of female martyrs.

It was easier to evade my husband in the city and excuses as to where I'd been were more readily come by: "Oh, I just stopped at the cobbler's to see if he'd fixed that boot of yours"; "Well, I thought I'd go by the fishmonger's in case he had any of that sole you like so much." It was fun just thinking up the lies. Before too long I did get myself a 'paramour,' as they say. He turned out to be number four. Now that I think of it I suppose he had his snares set all along—he could see that I stood to inherit something and that my present millstone wouldn't last too long. But we did have a lovely time, as long as we were lovers. I liked sneaking away. He had a quaint little garret, not much bigger than his bed—but that's all the room we needed. Things were working out perfectly. But Fortune stepped in and struck my husband blind. His suspicions soon turned to violent jealousy, though I told him he was being unjust, that I was insulted. He clung to my arm and would not let go. He always had to know where I was. It was all I could do to get a message to my lover and ask him to wait for me. Unfortunately, he did....

My thoughts had carried me through a good part of the afternoon. The sun was getting low, and I was starting to feel hungry. I turned my mare back up to the road and rejoined my fellows, all of whom seemed to be on the verge of falling asleep: the monk was in the midst of some interminable gloomy, moral exercise. I thought this might be a good time to make first contact with Troilus, so I edged over to his side.

"I've been off by myself," I explained. "What have I missed?"

"Not much," he answered glumly. "Did you hear the prioress?"

"No," I replied. "To tell the truth, that's why I left."

He gave a bitter little chuckle. "That was a wise choice. Her performance was a maudlin mix of bigotry and sentimentality."

I was glad to hear him say so. If he'd been one of her admirers I would have given up on him then and there. "Then, after she finished, Geoffrey—he's the so-called poet—launched into a silly romance about a knight named Sir Thopas, with a face white as fine bread and lips red as a rose. Mercifully he was soon interrupted by Bailly, who told him point-blank that his "foul rhyming was not worth a turd." Geoffrey, who'd probably been having us on with Sir T., then commenced what seemed to be the world's longest tale about a good man named Melibee, his better wife named Prudence, and their struggles against the forces of evil. I'm sure there was a moral in there somewhere, but by the end we were in varying degrees of a doze. And I can assure you that thus far the monk has said nothing worth waking up for."

"Your patience has indeed been tried," I said. "How long has he been at it?"

"Oh, I've lost track of time by now. It's such a farce. He obviously doesn't believe a word of this tripe he's dishing out."

I was beginning to like Troilus and his wry sense of humour.

Rolling his great eyes around in his bald head, that selfsame monk was just then intoning about the tragic end of king Croesus—"thus with unexpected stroke," he said dolorously, nearly overpowered by his own wisdom, "will Fortune bring down the proud. Whenever men put their trust in her, she will desert them, and cover her bright face with a cloud." He took a long swig from his flask, and officiously clearing his throat, prepared to drone on.

Harry looked miserable. This tale-telling had been his idea, but from Troilus' report the afternoon had been a complete disaster. I suppose because of the monk's rank, and because he hadn't been able to stop the miller from pushing him aside yesterday, Harry thought he had no right to intervene now. It seemed we were doomed. But suddenly an unexpected saviour emerged.

"Stop!" exclaimed the knight. I silently blessed him. "Good sir, no more of this. What you've said about the fall of the mighty is surely true, but a little gravity is enough for most of us. It can be a comfort to hear the opposite as well—how a man may rise from a miserable state to a happy one, from woe to joy."

Harry beamed with relief. He was off the hook. "You're right," he said gratefully to the knight. And to the monk, "No more tragedy, sir; there's no fun in your tale. I nearly fell asleep from boredom and the clerks will tell you that without an audience a moral tale is useless."

"Amen," said Troilus under his breath.

"But perhaps you'd like to tell of something else? Of hunting perhaps?" I turned to Troilus, and our faces fell. How could Harry risk giving the monk another chance? But he was offended and declined in a huff.

"Amen," said I, a little too loudly. The monk bristled, but Troilus smiled.

Now we were in for a real treat. Mme. E's chaperone, Father John, said he would tell a tale: "And it must be a merry one, or you will blame me."

The monkish clouds that had been covering Fortune's face cleared away and we were warmed again by the good priest's cheer.

This is the tale of a poor but thrifty widow, who lives in a humble cottage with her daughters. Just now she has three cows, three sows, a sheep called Molly, and a flock of chickens. Chauntecleer is the cock; he is without equal. He crows the hour more truly than any clock. His comb is coral red, his bill black as jet, his legs and toes like azure. Of his seven wives his favourite is Pertelote.

This morning, though, Chauntecleer is out of sorts. He has had a terrible dream about a fearsome beast who was wanting to kill him. Dame Pertelote chastizes him for being a coward—bad dreams come from eating too much, she says, or from gas. What he needs is a laxative. Chauntecleer is stung. He replies with a number of learned stories about the prophetic quality of dreams and the woe that awaits those who ignore them. Nonetheless, so distracted is he by Pertelote's beauty, that he lets the dream pass from his mind.

Flying down from their perch, they search for corn. The cock feathers his beloved Pertelote some twenty times, and proudly struts about the yard on his toes. "Madame Pertelote, my world's bliss, listen to the birds' song, look at the fresh flowers—my heart rejoices."

But how quickly worldly joy is lost! All too soon Russell, that sly fox, breaks into the yard and hides himself amongst the cabbages—O false murderer!—Alas, that the cock was persuaded by his wife! For it was woman's advice that first brought us to woe, and forced Adam from paradise.

Even as he struts, singing more merrily than a mermaid, Chauntecleer's eye alights on the fox. Before he has a chance to flee, the fox speaks, assuring him that he's a friend—he's there because he so wants to hear him sing—his father sang so beautifully. Can Chauntecleer do as well? Beguiled by Russell's flattery, the cock stands high upon his toes, stretches out his neck, shuts his eyes and begins to crow. Out springs the fox, grabs Chauntecleer by the throat, throws him over his back and heads for the wood.

When his wives see what has happened they set up a cry greater than that of the Trojan women when their city was destroyed. The widow and her daughters hear the woeful cries of the hens. With a "Help!" and "Harrow!" and "Alas!" they set off in pursuit, accompanied by villagers with staves, various dogs, a cow, her calf and the hogs; the ducks quack, the geese fly up into the trees, the bees swarm out of their hives.

But it is Chauntecleer who saves himself. Feigning calm he says to the fox, "If I were you, I'd say 'Turn back, you churls! A pestilence upon you!'" The fox replies, "In faith, I shall." But, as he opens his mouth to speak, Chauntecleer breaks free and flies high up into a tree. Russell tries to lure him down, but the cock has learned his lesson. "Nay," he says, "you shall trick me no more. God grant that whoever willingly closes his eyes when they should be open may never prosper!" "And," replies the fox, "ill luck to him who is so careless as to chatter when he ought to keep his mouth shut!"

Now, good Lord, if it be your will, make us all virtuous and bring us to bliss! Amen.

Cheers and laughter greeted the end of the priest's story. He had indeed kept his promise—it was exactly what the knight had asked for—a tale of joy after woe, to counter the monk's gloom. Except to the vanity of the cock, no damage had been done. Chauntecleer and his adoring wives could live happily ever after. All the good widow's chickens were safe. She'd also discovered—down to the very bees—the devotion of her barnyard; and it would surely not be long before the crafty Russell managed to find himself another meal, albeit one less tasty.

We'd expected to arrive at Ospringe in a state of desperate boredom. Instead we were chattering and cheering, ready for a revel. The delicious fragrance of roast goose greeted us as we dismounted outside the inn. Happily it wasn't chicken, or we might have had reason to doubt the optimism of the nun's priest.

جﮯ

Eglentyne. We were served a lovely stuffed goose at Ospringe— but I had such butterflies in my stomach that I could hardly eat. I did manage to sneak a glass of wine, but it only made me more trembly. As Richard came towards me I could feel a flush spreading over my cheeks and the more flustered I felt the pinker I got. Well, what was the point of trying to hide my feelings? He might as well know!

"Good evening, Eglentyne, " he said, bowing slightly. "I hope you are still willing for us to have our talk?" I nodded, and rose.

"It is so hot, and so loud in here," he went on, "that I hoped we might walk outside in the garden, and enjoy the evening." I wondered what my priest would say, and looked over towards him. No problem there! He'd told the last tale that afternoon, a fable of Chauntecleer the cock, how he was captured by Russell the fox and then was able to escape. I'd hardly listened but the other pilgrims obviously loved it. He was the hero of the evening, surrounded by admirers who were refilling his glass as quickly as he could empty it. He certainly wasn't going to notice, or care, if I walked outside. Sister Cecilia of course had already gone upstairs to say her prayers.

It was cool and fragrant in the garden, but quite dark, so Richard offered me his arm. I didn't know if it was proper but I couldn't say no to him and I did feel quite shaky, so I took it. I could feel the warmth of his strong arm right through his tunic. I thought this might be the most wonderful moment of my life.

"Thank you, Richard," I managed to say, trying to steady my voice. "You are very kind."

"On the contrary," he replied, " the kindness is all yours in coming out with me and being willing to listen."

"What was it you wanted to say?"

"I hardly know where to begin," he answered. "Perhaps I should say, first of all, how much I admire you." My heart was in my throat. "I hope this is not an affront to a lady in your position. I have been away so long I hardly know what is correct, but I must speak the truth. Eglentyne, you are delicate and sensitive, and I have to say, to my eyes very beautiful." I started to speak (I knew I should say something modest) but he stopped me. "Please, don't be angry. I know there is no way you can return my regard"—if only he knew of my yearning towards him!—"but there are so many things I want to say and you have a right to know why I have presumed to ask for your time."

I had no idea how to react. I knew that courtly ladies were supposed to be disdainful—but then I was hardly in Guenivere's situation—and as a religious I thought I should be at least a little sympathetic. Finally I managed to say, "Please Richard, feel free to open your heart to me." I hoped he realized this was not just charity speaking.

"For many years," he began, "I've been away far more than I've been here in England. When I went on my first crusade I was young and full of idealism. After all I'd been named for the first Richard, the great crusading king, so I thought I knew what my life's path should be. I did know that Jerusalem had long ago been lost to the pagans, but still I hoped to be part of winning it back, of helping to build a united Christendom. Though we fought in Asia Minor, we got nowhere near the holy land, but I was not discouraged. Finally I came home and was married. I hardly knew my new wife, as we'd been chosen for each other by our parents. Still, I came to care for her"—I began to dread he'd say she was waiting patiently for him back at the manor—"especially when I learned that she was with child. She was so young, but she was pretty, with grey eyes very like yours. I do believe she was fond of me too, though we never knew how to speak of such things, and then so quickly she was gone."

"Gone?" I asked, trying not to sound hopeful.

"Yes, she died in childbirth, bringing forth the fine young man who's with me now. I grieved her loss, though now I don't imagine I truly loved her, but worse, I felt guilty that my act had brought about her death. I thought I might have waited until she was older and stronger, and not just doing her wifely duty."

"Oh, Richard, how sad for you," I said, trying myself to sound sad. But I was relieved. I didn't have to hope for her death, and after all I wasn't in love (there, I've said it!) with a man who was married. But where did that leave me as a prioress? I was muddled but too happy to care. "Please, do go on."

"Well, the wee lad was fair and healthy from the start. I had no fears for him. I left him with my mother, who absolutely doted on him—just to look at him you can see how well cared-for he's been—and went off on another crusade. Well, it was battle after battle. Sometimes the Saracens won and sometimes we did. Always there was bloodshed and more bloodshed, bodies littering the field, the air filled with the moaning of the wounded, the grass red with blood. I was beginning to find the whole business ugly. It seemed so useless. To make matters worse I heard some stories about king Richard that shook my loyalty."

I was surprised by this. "What did you hear?"

"Well, I'll just give you one example. I don't want to shock you, but once he ordered thousands of captives executed, simply because their ransom was not paid on time, though the pagans had kept their promise and released the Christian prisoners. No matter how I tried I could not but see this as cowardly. Those men were helpless, they could not defend themselves.

"After a time I had a chance to move to the front in Prussia, and fight with the Teutonic Order. I had heard of their military prowess and hoped things would be better. But they were worse. It was not a fight for Christendom, as far as I could see. All they wanted was to expand their power and set themselves up as a ruling aristocracy. And their brutality against the pagans was like nothing I had seen before. They killed everyone they could get their hands on. Not just the soldiers, but the women and children too. They'd go into a village and set the huts on fire, then cut them down as they ran out. Sometimes they would capture the women and make them watch while their children were killed, then they'd take them back to their camp and.... I can't bear to tell you what they did to the women, but when they'd finished, they killed them too.

"I didn't know what to do. I knew it was not necessary to kill pagan prisoners, that it was possible to convert them and save their souls for God. I didn't take part, but it wasn't enough to keep silent. A few times I tried to intervene. At first they thought I just wanted the women for myself. To them that was all right. They were always quarrelling amongst themselves as to who should get the prettier ones, or the ones who tried to fight back. When my fellow soldiers realized that I wanted to protect the women they were at first incredulous—didn't I know that pagan women had no honour to preserve?—and then enraged. They turned on me. I tried to defend myself but they were twenty at least to my one. They knocked away my sword and proceeded to slash and kick at me and left me as dead next to the heap of their mutilated victims. Then they went back to battle."

I was horrified. I'd never heard anything but good about the crusades. "Richard, this is terrible," I cried. "Why are you telling me this? Can it be true?"

"Eglentyne, I beg your pardon. I ought to have been more considerate of your tenderness. I know you have lived a protected life in the convent, that the horrors of the world have been kept from you. But there are reasons for my telling. I esteem you and I want you to know me, the real me, not just some romantic idea you have about knights. I have been brave, but I have also been cowardly. I have killed for the so-called glory of God. I have killed because it was a job. I have killed because I was too cowardly to be killed myself. Can you understand that? I must know if you can have any feeling for me now that you know the truth."

The fact was that Richard's story left me in a terrible state. What he said went against everything I'd ever been taught. But he was the most earnest, truthful person I had ever met. With his beautiful sad eyes he pleaded with me to believe him. It seemed that no one before had ever really cared about how I felt—they'd only wanted me to play a part and follow the rules. I felt my heart going out to him. I wanted to take him in my arms. My world was upside down.

"Richard, I do believe you. You are honourable, you are true.... But this is so hard for me."

"Yes, dear Eglentyne, it is hard. There are some terrible things about our world. Please pardon me for hurting you, but I must go on. You have been stifled in that convent. You have been kept away from the horror, but also the beauty, of this life. You have been kept from becoming the woman you should be, that I know you can be!"

"Richard, take care," I said, but my head was swimming with his words. How many times had I said such things to myself? How often had I longed for someone like Richard?

He hung his head. "Forgive me. I will say no more. I have already gone too far."

This was the last thing I wanted.

"No, Richard," I said quickly, "it is I you must forgive. I have been so ignorant. I know nothing. It's just that this is so sudden, but I do want to hear more. No one but you has ever been honest with me. It's too late now—don't leave me alone with these terrible stories."

"Dear Eglentyne," he said—and turning, clasped my hands. Now we were looking full into each other's eyes. "Thank you. There is still more, but dare I go on?"

"Yes, oh, yes, Richard, please," I begged. Tears filled my eyes.

I was afraid. I wanted to stay with him. I thought I could never go back to being the lonely, smiling prioress. She seemed like a far-off stranger. We walked on and again I took his arm.

"All right, if you're sure. After my Teutonic brethren went off I dragged myself to a nearby brook. I drank and splashed water on some of my wounds. I knew I had to get away before they returned. I staggered to my feet, gathered some supplies from the camp and moved painfully off in the opposite direction, away from the frontier. I had money and was able to buy rides in a succession of peasant carts. Finally I reached a Christian city, where I hoped to be safe and to get medical attention for some of my wounds had become putrid. To my horror, the citizens turned their backs on me. They said I was a traitor—a heretic! Why had I left the front? I ought to die in the street, like a dog. I belonged with the moneylending Jews, who also followed Satan.

"Like you, Eglentyne, I had been brought up to hate and fear the Jews. I too had been told the stories of how they murdered Christian children. I thought I would rather die in a Christian street, but the good citizens would not let me. They took up cudgels and drove me to the Jewish quarter, where I expected to be tortured and carved into pieces.

"But no, to my amazement the Jews took me in. Though they knew I was a crusader, what they saw was a broken, hopeless man. They fed me, they tended my wounds. I couldn't ask them why. Their language was so strange. Maybe they knew I'd deserted. I don't say that they liked me, or that they wanted me to stay—they didn't. When I was strong enough they put me on a mule and sent me on my way. But while I was with them I could see that they're really no different than we are—no horns, no cloven feet, no bread made of Christian blood. They love their families, they love their god, they have dignity, honour, their own way of life.

"As I made my way I was filled with shame, with the sense that my whole life had been based on a lie. I vowed that as soon as I got back to England I would make a pilgrimage, and try to atone for my wrongs. I was afraid that my faith would never again be strong enough to overcome my terrible despair."

"Richard," I whispered. "You mustn't blame yourself. You tried to do what was right and you have suffered for it. I knew from your face that there had been sadness in your life—but I never thought it could be this bad. I think you are very noble. Compared to yours my life has been so easy. Yet I've complained, and been vain, and thought only of myself. And I told that story. I pretended it was mine, but really it was just one I'd heard from passing friars. I did believe the Jews were evil, though I don't know why. I've never met one in my life. But, and this is the worst part, I chose it because I wanted you to think well of me, I thought it would make you like me more."

"Eglentyne, thank you for telling me the truth. In your tale, when you got to the part about the Jews, I knew it wasn't yours. I've heard many like it before. It's the kind of story that's told to soldiers to work them up, to convince them they're acting for God when they're slaughtering infidels. I knew it wasn't yours. There now, don't cry."

Tears were streaming down my face. "But I told it, and how bad does that make me?" Now he knows what a hypocrite I am, I thought, now I've lost him.

"When I heard the tale," he said gently, "I heard two things. One, that you'd been fed false stories meant to poison your mind, and that you'd been shut up so that you'd never know they were not real. But I also heard your true self when you told about the mother's grief. There was such sweet feeling for her. I could tell you were capable of real compassion and ... can I say it? I thought you were grieving for the child you were never able to have."

"Oh, Richard," I said, "I do love you." I didn't mean to say it, but there it was. After all this truth how could I not say it? It was so dark I could not see his face. Did he despise me now? No woman, religious or otherwise, was meant to speak so. He was quiet. I supposed he was thinking of how he could get away, now that he knew how bad I was. Finally he led me to a bench by a flowering hawthorn and we sat. The air was soft. The night birds had begun to sing. I clung to his arm and wept.

"Dear Eglentyne, excuse me, I am overcome. I never dreamed that such happiness would ever be possible for me. I have been the cause of so many deaths—my poor child-wife, who I never even loved, so many pagans—it seemed that the best I could do would be to spend my remaining years in penance. Now you have offered this beautiful gift to me. Of course I can never hope for more. It would be wrong to want it. But to know you love me, just to know that, will take me peacefully to the end of my days."

I was at a loss, again. I thought he must be right. There was no sense in wanting more. I was bound to that convent for life. I hoped he wasn't going to be content never to see me again and just to love me from afar. I tried to think if my sisters had ever told me stories in which, though the lovers had to live separately, they were happy just in the knowledge of each other's love. I couldn't remember any. I didn't think there could be. I was sure I couldn't manage it.

"My dear," he said sadly, "it is late, and I should be taking you in." I wanted to stay here forever. Cecilia wouldn't miss me. She'd have been fast asleep for hours, dreaming happily of martyrdom. "But before we go in, we have come so far, can I ask one more thing?" Was I going to say no to anything?

"Of course, dear Richard."

"Would you ... would you ...is it possible for you to take off your wimple?"

Now I knew this was absolutely forbidden, but then, so was much of our talk. I wondered if I should be afraid of God. Would I be struck down, or marked with the pox, if I agreed? For a moment I hesitated. On the one side there were my years—decades—in the safety of the convent, where all the rules were known, where everyone looked up to me and, on the other, there was Richard. I reached up and untied the laces.

"You may take it off, Richard. I'd be glad for you to take it off." Carefully he lifted it away from my head and gazed at me quietly in the shadows. I sat very still, thinking I'd never felt this beautiful before. The evening breeze was soft on my neck. Then slowly he raised his hand to my hair and passed two strokes over it, and then another, gentle as a feather, but still there was the warmth of his hand.

"Eglentyne, I have seen so much horror, been so alone, felt such despair, but this ... this seems to take away all the pain." His voice was thick. "Bless you." And so we went in.

ॐ

The revel at Ospringe went on long after the last bone of the last roast goose had been licked clean, the wine and ale flowing freely. A few tipsy minstrels led us in some decidedly unholy songs of the road— "welcome Bacchus, glorious god," "we made our bed beneath the bowers," and so forth. With each of the many puns about cocks rising in the morning, mugs were raised to father John, saviour of the day. He sat in the midst of his adoring circle, utterly unperturbed by the gleeful ribaldry and looking very rosy. Having travelled and supped together the last few days, overcoming such hardships as fleas, mud and monkish gloom, most of the pilgrims seemed to feel they'd been friends forever. Tonight was for pleasure. Tomorrow meant Canterbury and at least the pretence of piety.

I wasn't surprised to see the homely nun slip upstairs as soon as she could, and of course Troilus had already escaped to the attic. The parson, a little rosy himself, stood nervously aside, trying to hide his smiles as the bawdy jokes flew by. The monk sulked briefly, but was too fond of his food and drink to hold out for long. Robyn lurched over to Oswald and swore they must be friends. By God's bones wouldn't he share his pitcher of ale (of which a great deal had already been consumed) with him? Len was several sheets to the wind, clutching the table for support. He wouldn't be a problem tonight. The lawyer sat stiffly apart doing his best to look dignified, but no one paid him any mind. Though Harry was busily filling and refilling mugs, he glanced my way often enough that I knew he was looking forward to our meeting. But where were Mme. E. and her swain? Not in evidence. I knew they wouldn't be upstairs, let alone behind the barrels in the hall, but where else could they be? They were getting positively foxy. I'd have to keep an eye out for them.

For now I had other fish to fry. During the meal I'd wrapped up a few dainties—figs, oysters, sweetmeats—and slipped them into one pocket. Into another went two goblets and a little platter. Under my arm I cradled a bottle of Spanish red. I went up the stairs, casual as could be and then burst out laughing as I skipped along to my little room. It had one chair, which, setting out the treats, I quickly turned into a table lest Harry in a mistaken gesture of gentlemanliness felt he should sit there instead of on the bed. Back down the hall I paid a visit to the men's bedroom, helping myself to the lawyer's candles and the merchant's cushions. On the way out I noticed the monk's fur-lined cloak and grabbed that up as well. I was sure he wouldn't notice its absence tonight. I spread the cloak fur-side up over my bed, setting the cushions against the wall. The candles I put here and there, sprinkling into them a bit of cinnamon, to sweeten the air.

Stepping back, I had to admire my handiwork. The plain little room had been transformed into a magical courtly chamber. There was still the problem of the window, but that was easily solved. Taking off my outer riding skirt (which would save time later anyhow), I went over to hang it from the casement, and who should I see in the garden below? Eglentyne and Braveheart! It was dark, but not too dark for me to see that they were standing very close, holding each others' hands! The little vixen! How far would she go? I wished I could wait to see what would happen next, but Harry was a far more tempting prospect. Given the choice I'd certainly rather make my own love than watch someone else's. So I let the curtain fall on that little drama and went back down to the dining hall.

Harry beamed, and strode over to greet me. "Alison," he said, "where have you been? I've looked everywhere. I thought..." and here he hesitated and looked down, reddening, "I ... I was afraid you might have forgotten about our ... our plan." I was touched. It hadn't occurred to me to play hard to get, but my sojurn upstairs had had the same effect—he was keener than ever.

"No, Harry. No, no. It's just that I could see you were busy for the time, and the jokes were beginning to wear thin. So I went to my room for a bit."

Here I was a little less than honest. Most times I would leap at the chance to carouse with a tavern crowd, and took pride in being able to sing the bawdiest ballads and drink everyone under the table. Harry needn't know this, but I didn't want him to start seeing me as another Mme. E., either. So I smiled at him and said, "Look, Harry. It's too noisy here, it's too bright, it's too crowded, and I don't fancy a walk in the garden" (for more reasons than he knew). "Why don't you come up to my room?"

"Why, that would be splendid, Alison. I do believe my work here is done." (Those who could still walk were freely helping themselves at the taps, and weaving back with reinforcements to their bench-bound fellows.) We crept upstairs.

Harry was as pleased with the room as I'd hoped.

"Why Alison, this is just lovely. How did you ever manage this? It's like a dream come true. I can't believe it."

"Well," I said, "I wanted us to be comfortable while we talked." I noticed that Harry was looking around uncertainly.

"There's no chair, Harry. I'm sorry about that, but I had to turn it into a table. You'll have to sit here beside me, but don't worry, it's not a bed anymore, I've turned it into a sort of divan, like the Saracens have, for sitting on. I saw them when I was in the holy land. They're much better than our wooden chairs and benches, really. Try it."

Harry sat gingerly on the edge.

"No—you have to sit back. Give yourself over to it, Harry. Lean against the cushions. Put your feet up. That's right. How does it feel?" He was starting to smile.

I went on. "The problem with England is that comfort is only supposed to be for the upper classes. You can believe they have plenty of soft stuff to sit upon. Well, just for tonight, Harry, I'd like to pretend that you are royalty. You deserve it. Soon enough we'll both be back at work." He moved a little deeper into the cushions.

"It does feel wonderful, Alison, I have to admit. I guess those pagans aren't all bad."

"Right, and now let me serve you. You've been waiting on every one else all night, and taking care of us on the road. It's your turn." I filled up the goblets, offering one to him and taking the other. "Let's drink to each other, to our time together."

Harry drank and needless to say so did I. "Now we have to get really comfortable. Give me your foot." He did, and I took off his boot. I looked meaningfully at his other foot, and he gave it to me. I took off the other boot, and set them both on the floor. "Now, isn't that better?" He had a funny look on his face.

"Now I'll just rub your feet a bit. You must be tired from all that running around downstairs. Here, have something to eat." I passed him the platter of treats and started working on his feet. He took a few of the oysters and sighed with pleasure.

After a while a shadow came over his face. "But Alison, this isn't fair. What about you?"

"Oh, you get to take my shoes off, too, Harry," I said, and draped an ankle across his knee. He fumbled a bit with my shoe, but soon had it off.

"Now for the other?" he asked. "Please."

"You don't have to be so polite, Harry," I said, placing the other ankle a little higher on his thigh, and showing off a bit more leg, "this one will be easier." And sure enough he slipped it right off and set the pair next to his boots on the floor.

"And shall I rub your feet as well?" he asked.

"As you like, milord. But first I have a favour to ask. Will you please let my hair down? It's so uncomfortable piled up like this." I turned and arched my neck back towards him. "Just pull out those pins."

He did, one at a time, quite timidly, but finally my thick auburn hair came tumbling down, right to my waist. I heard Harry let out his breath. "Oh, thank you, Harry. You can't imagine how good that feels. Now you can do my feet." My feet are not exactly delicate, but in his huge hands they seemed so. He stroked them ever so softly, as if he feared they would break. It felt glorious. I didn't want it to stop.

"Oh, I forgot!" he suddenly said, and passed me the plate. I tried a fig and an oyster together, a lovely combination, sweet and smoky.

"Now," he said, still keeping one big warm hand gently round my feet, "now, let me guess, it's time for another drink to each other. Am I right?"

"An excellent plan, milord." So we drank, and worked some more on the figs and oysters.

"One more favour, though. Would you mind brushing out my hair?" Without waiting for an answer, I handed him the brush, and he began to run it through my hair. Now I have to say that I find having my feet stroked and my hair brushed utterly exquisite. The air was heady, fragrant with cinnamon. The wine was warming my blood. I was beginning to tingle. Maybe I was going a bit too fast. We were supposed to talk, after all, and I didn't want it to be over too soon. One Len was enough for this trip.

"And now, am I right," asked Harry a little hoarsely, "now you get to brush my hair?" He was catching on. Slowing down was going to be a challenge.

"Very good, milord. But for me to do that you'll have to put your head in my lap. You're so tall, I won't be able to reach your hair otherwise."

He obeyed and I slowly ran the brush through his thick locks, spreading them out over my lap. Harry's eyes were closed, and he was breathing deeply. "Now you don't look so much like a lord as a god from the other world. What a fine forehead you have," I said, stroking back his hair. Harry gasped and reached up for me. The brush went flying. He wrapped his great arms around me and I forgot about the talking. I worked at the ties on his shirt and soon had it open, running my fingers through the rich mat of hair on his chest. With a little help from me we soon had my bodice off and I fell into the fur. It was wonderful against my back.

"Wait, Harry, "I laughed, "you have to feel this. Take off

your shirt." He tore it over his head and threw it across the room. We wrapped our arms around each other, delighting in the feel of skin on skin, revelling in the plushness of the cloak, whose unsuspecting owner proceeded with his stupefaction below.

"Harry," I managed to whisper, as we struggled with the rest of our clothes, "Let's take our time."

"That's fine ... with ... me," he said, catching his breath. So we did, and it was grand. One of those times when the pleasure of the journey was such it was almost a pity to reach the destination. Afterwards, we finished what was left of the wine and the sweetmeats. A sort of dessert.

I suppose neither of us really wanted to break the spell, but falling asleep didn't seem like a very interesting alternative.

"Harry," I finally said, "I thought we were going to talk."

"Yes, of course, Alison, sorry. Of course, that's why I'm here, isn't it? I guess I've been awfully selfish."

"No more than I have," I replied, surprising myself with my frankness. "And in truth, milord, I've loved every minute. But still I'd like to know more about you."

"Why, thank you, but why don't you go first? I want to hear your story too." I obliged, and gave him a shortened account of the unholy trinity, how young I'd been, how they'd used and abused me. I didn't think I needed to mention my extracurricular dalliances, but did tell him about number four's infidelities, and Jankyn's sudden death. By the time I'd finished, Harry's face and beard were wet with tears.

"Oh, my dear Alison, that's terrible! Terrible!" He took my hand and pressed it against his wet cheek. "I wish the world knew of such things. You know, I think you'll have to tell your tale first thing tomorrow—or is it today by now? Perhaps others who have daughters may learn from your sad experience." I privately doubted that too many girls would be saved by my story. From all I knew, their commercial value most always outweighed parental devotion. But I was pleased at the prospect of having my turn, being the centre of attention and shocking the prigs. I thought about this a moment.

"Harry," I said, "don't be surprised if tomorrow's version is a little spicier than what I've told you. You know, I don't want to be depressing. And it'll be a challenge to penetrate all those hangovers."

"Of course, dear Alison. Whatever you want. I'm so pleased that you've been able to confide in me tonight."

I felt a pang of conscience, but what could I do? I *had* told Harry the truth, just not all of it. I squeezed his hand. "And now, please tell me your story."

"I hardly know how to start," he said sadly. "I don't want to be depressing either, but there's no way around it. The fact is that my marriage has been hell on earth. My wife, Goodelief, 'dear good one,' now that's a joke—despises me. I don't know how else to put it. I don't know what she wants from me. It's true I'm not rich, but I work hard and get her whatever I can afford. We have no children. Soon after we were married she declared me a failure in bed and would have no more of that."

"I promise you she's dead wrong there," I interposed.

"Well, I can't say I enjoyed it either, she was so cold and complained all the way through. But I would dearly have loved a few little ones to brighten my days. She insults me at home, telling me I'm useless and a weakling. If one of our servants disobeys and I have to use the switch—which I hate to do—she brings me a staff and shouts "break their backs!" When I refuse she calls me a milksop and wonders why God has sent her such a miserable creature for a husband. If someone at church does not treat her with what she sees as the respect she deserves she cries out in front of everyone that I'm a coward, an ape, who dares not defend his own wife. She says she should take the knife, and leave me the spindle, to do a woman's work. What she would like is for me to fight my neighbour, and slay him, to restore her honour. She gets me so worked up, so humiliated that I'm afraid some day I will. Of course I hate the thought, but I hate her insults more—they burn into me. Sometimes I find myself believing her; maybe I am as worthless as she says. Sometimes I even wonder if she might despise me less if I did the 'manly' thing

and broke the servants' bones, or killed someone for her sake.
But then I realize it would do no good. I would hate myself, my
life would be destroyed and she'd still hate me too."

Now *I* was crying. This Goodelief was making me look like a
saint, and that took some doing. I had been hard on the unholy
trinity, but they'd offended first, and they'd been nothing like
the man Harry was, sensitive, gentle, courteous—a rare enough
combination and, on top of all that, a warm, generous lover. I
wondered briefly what my life would have been like if he'd been
my first husband—but that would not have been possible—my
father must go for the best offer, get the highest price. I knew I'd
survived by growing an ever thicker skin, by learning to laugh
and learning to lie. I wondered how Harry had managed.

"Harry, oh Harry," I cried, and hugged him to me. "How is
it possible you are still so sweet? How can you live with such pain
and not be angry?" I really wanted to know.

"Oh, Alison," he replied, holding me closer, "I'm not so wonderful. Don't forget I'm a man, and have more freedom that you
did. To tell the truth, the reason I offered to come on this pilgrimage was to get away from home. My position at the Tabard
often allows me to get away. Now don't think there are other
women—you may believe it or not, but you're the first, and after
our wonderful night I don't mind if you're the last.

"No, I go with the pilgrims when I can, and I try ... I try to
pull them together, to head off grievances, to make sure they
have a good time, love one another if they can, be healed of
their hurts, feel somehow—it's different with each one—but somehow better about themselves and their lives for having come to
Canterbury. And you know, it's not so bad. There's a lot of grati-
tude. People realize I've made a difference, and then that makes
me see that Goodelief must be wrong, there are other ways to be
strong than to go after someone with a knife. And I do see them
feeling better. Many a time, most times, pilgrims think they are
just going for a lark, but they are changed—almost despite themselves—by this journey. There's something about it that moves
people, makes them more open, more able to love.... I don't know

how else to describe it. But for me, to be a part of it makes life worth living, you might almost say, restores my faith. So there you have it, Alison. I hope *you* don't think me an ape."

"Hardly, milord, you're as fine as a man can be." I hugged him some more, and we lay down beneath the monk's fur and cried together until we slept, close in one another's arms.

ॐ

Day Three

*E*glentyne. When we came in from the garden Richard bade me a solemn farewell at the foot of the stairs, as if we'd never talk again. I knew he thought he'd said too much, that he'd been wrong to show his feelings for me. I certainly knew I'd gone too far. It tore at my heart to part from him, but I didn't see what else I could do. The sad fact was that I had taken those vows, though I hadn't wanted to. I was pledged to the religious life, and as a prioress was far more trapped than I'd been as a novice. Being on this pilgrimage was as free as I was ever going to be. I'd grown used to the convent, but now I knew more than ever how unhappy I was there, that it was not the life for me. Richard was right. It had kept me from being the woman I should have been, from being a woman at all.

As I crept back into my room, afraid of waking Cecilia, I was faint with confusion. What Richard and I both wanted was wrong. I knew that from everything I'd been taught since the day I first entered the convent. The thrill I'd felt when he looked in my eyes, when he'd stroked my hair—oh, when he'd stroked my hair!—that was a sin. I got into bed, but knew I could not sleep. Tristan and Isolde jumped up beside me and anxiously licked my face. I stroked their little bodies and they were consoled, but I was not. Now I could see that I loved them in place of the children I would never have. I felt a burning sense of shame—the first time I'd ever had that feeling. I'd been so used to thinking of myself as perfect, and now I saw that was a sin as well. I remembered all the times I'd made myself charming so as to control the men I'd had to deal with, how I'd enjoyed their adoration and my power over them. That was a sin. I was a miserable creature. I'd heard so many sermons about sinners, how they angered God, how they would be punished in hell, and I'd always felt so superior. I even thought I'd probably be one of those who went straight to heaven, I'd been so noble just putting up with that boring convent.

Now I burned with shame; but even more I burned with longing for Richard. I knew that really virtuous women—like Constance—did not feel this way, even after they were married. I thought of Saint Cecilia (the real one), who convinced her new husband to live a life of chastity. What did that make me? The worst kind of sinner. Whatever wrong Richard had committed by wanting me was my fault too. Perhaps God had sent him as a temptation —and how had I reacted? I hadn't even tried to resist. The idea of a hair shirt had never crossed my mind. I had failed.

And still I longed for him. Even after my great sin I felt no contrition. That made me even worse. I knew I would never admit to my feelings, or to what had passed between us, in confession, which would mean that any communion I took from now on would be false. God would never forgive that. I began to see that my pride, and my lust—yes, that's what it was, why try to deny it?—would doom me to one of the lowest circles of hell. Well, I could try to work on the pride, I could stop trying to be so charming. I could try not to grumble when we had to get up for midnight prayers. I could stop showing off my forehead and stop wearing my lovely bracelet. No, not lovely, wicked. But I knew I could not stop wanting Richard. I wept, and I felt my sin, but I could not stop the longing. I could not repent.

At last the dawn came. Cecilia stirred, rose, and knelt by her bed in silent prayer. She looked up in surprise as I fell to my knees beside her. I thought I might at least pray for contrition, but it did not come. I put my arm through hers, hoping that some of her reverence might pass over to me, but it was no use. I loved him.

We got up together and put on our habits. I pulled my wimple down over my brow and left my bracelet, with its 'amor vincit omnia' glaring accusingly at me from the bedside table. We went

71

down together, arm-in-arm. She said nothing, but I could tell she was pleased at what seemed to be my new piety. We sat at our little table by the window, apart from the others. I did not look up. I knew Richard was there, but I could not meet his gaze. By now he must have come to his senses and realized just how bad I really was. I watched Cecilia, eating only what she ate—a little bread and some cold water. I pushed the rest away. Quietly we waited for Father John, who was quite a while in coming down. When he did join us he sat for a time with his head in his hands, as if he were in pain. After a bit he said he was sorry, and asked the servant for a pint of ale. That seemed to make him feel a little better. He toyed with his food, but didn't seem to have much of an appetite either. Finally he gave up, and led us in a little prayer asking God to forgive our trespasses. Fervently, though for very different reasons, we all three said amen.

Gradually the other pilgrims straggled in—a sorry lot, except for the lawyer, who walked about casting disdainful glances at his comrades, many of whom looked quite ill. I stayed with Cecila, keeping my eyes on the floor. Perhaps if Richard believed me to be repentant he might not lose all respect for me. And if I could conceal my longing, perhaps God would not be so very angry with me. So except for an occasional groan from Father John we sat in silence, awaiting the hour of departure.

⁂

I woke up feeling better than I'd felt for a year, since I'd lost Jankyn. Harry had left before sun-up, taking the cloak with him. I supposed the monk would wonder at the odd bit of sticky sweetmeat he'd find here and there in its fur, but he'd never guess where it had spent the night. I sprang out of bed and dressed to look my best. As I took my riding skirt down from the window I remembered the little tryst I'd spied in the garden below and wondered how those two lovers had fared.

The sun shone into my window, a good omen. I was going to lead off with my story, and was already working out various ways to scandalize my audience. I thought I'd spend some time telling them about my own life, including every possible outrageous detail, and throwing in a few imaginary ones for good measure. I'd have to begin with some blasphemy. That would be sure to get their attention and would lead up nicely to the portrait of myself as a gleeful reprobate. Thanks to Jankyn's book (the one we burned) I knew pretty much by heart all the evils women were supposed to be guilty of—lechery of course, but also false-hood, greed, envy, vanity—what else?—oh yes, inconstancy and disobedience. We were, after all, the devil's gateway, responsible for Adam's fall, leading men who would otherwise be chaste into temptation (poor souls!) and, because of us, God had to send his only son to be crucified. I planned to claim, and flaunt, every one of these vices as my own.

But what should I tell as a tale? Perhaps something to out-bawd the bawdy miller? I'd give that some thought. Downstairs I headed for the privy, but stopped outside the door. Did I really want to closet myself in that smelly little chamber where prob-ably half the hung-over pilgrims had already been pissing that morning? No. It was the great outdoors for me. I skipped into the sunlight, across the road and through the hedge, down a slope into a pretty glade encircled by little greening trees. Prim-roses dotted the grass, over to one side was a cluster of blue-bells, on another a whole bank of early daisies—for me, today, truly the day's eyes—dancing in the morning sun. I didn't see how my water could improve on nature's showers, so I chose a patch of ferns that looked pretty hardy.

"Ferns," I said, "please take this in the spirit in which it is meant, as a sort of baptism, or at the very least a sign of camara-derie. Tough as you are, you're more like me than those tender blossoms. Please accept my offering." I hoisted my skirts and squatted down, the fern-tendrils softly tickling my thighs, the warm April breeze caressing my bum. I thought that pissing when one's bladder was full had to be one of the greatest, most underappreciated pleasures God had sent us—it was something to be truly grateful for. So I said a little prayer.

"Thank you God, for giving us the power to piss. We see how the animals, though they are supposedly inferior to us, know how to rejoice in it. We see how each does it in his (or her) own way. The tomcat will piss on a bush, challenging his rivals to battle. The female cat will dig a hole and coyly bury her puddle—but not too deep—knowing its lingering scent will catch the attention of the tom. The stallion and the mare alike will both let it out in a joyous torrent. Blithely lifting his leg, the dog will piss to mark his territory, hoping to impress the bitch who has squatted to achieve her more bashful, but no less pleasurable, release. So thank you. And amen." I then let flow my own eager stream, feeling a kind of joy that for this moment at least I was one with the creation, that at this moment God the Father and the Goddess Natura were one, as they should always be, but as in the poor, guilt-ridden human world, they almost never were.

"Thank you, friends," I said to the ferns, and headed back for some breakfast. I was hugely hungry.

It took awhile to assemble the pilgrims, most of whom were varying shades of green. I looked about for Mme. E. and her knight. They seemed to be keeping as far apart as possible. Both looked pale as ghosts and utterly miserable. Something must have gone wrong. While I would have preferred to gloat, I found that I was slightly sorry for them. It was an odd feeling.

At last we were all in our saddles—though some looked distinctly dubious as to their balance—and started down the road towards Bobbe-up-and-down, from whence it was but a short ride to Canterbury. Harry, looking only a little bleary, called the pilgrims to order and announced that I was to tell the first tale. I'd been counting on E. to stick her adorable nose in the air, or show her indignation in some other prissy way, but she hardly seemed aware of me. Well, I'd just have to concentrate on offending the men instead.

I started out as planned, telling of my five marriages, quoting and misquoting scripture to defend myself against the charge of bigamy, and comparing myself to Solomon and his many wives—"the first night *he* had a merry time with each of them!" I pointed out—and taking particular aim at that old fart St. Paul— "after all, *he* said it was better to marry than to burn." Abraham, I argued reasonably, and Jacob, both holy men, had more than two wives.

Where, I asked, had God commanded virginity? Men may counsel women to be pure, but advice is no commandment. If God had wanted us all to be maidens, there would be no weddings. "And I ask you," I said, in what I thought was a rather brilliant bit of logic, "if no seeds are sown, from whence should other virgins grow? I'm sure Paul was a maid," I added, "but even he would not dare command a thing his master had not ordered."

I allowed that perhaps virginity is the greatest perfection; "but a man does not want every vessel in his house to be of gold. Some must be of wood and be useful to their lord. For that matter, barley bread is far better for us than that made of pure white flour." I was borne along by the momentum of my wit. "God calls people to him in many ways. Christ did not tell everyone to give what they had to the poor: he spoke only to those who would live perfectly."

If God did not want us to marry, I continued, "why then has he given us our organs of generation? Well may you argue that they are for the purgation of urine, and to allow us to distinguish between man and woman. But experience tells us there's more—how should a man yield his wife her debt if he does not use his blessed instrument? In wifehood," I boasted, "I will use *mine* as freely as my maker has given it."

This was too much for the pardoner—one of the more motley ecclesiasts—who started forward and cried, "Madame, you are indeed a noble preacher. I was about to marry, but now I've thought better of it. Why should I pay so dearly with the price of my flesh?" (And who, I said to myself, would want any part of your ugly body?) But I was pleased to be stirring up some trouble. So I proceeded with the details of my marriages, dwelling on how repulsive I found my old husbands, how I tormented them with accusations of infidelity lest they should discover mine, and finishing up with how happy Jankyn and I had been after he decided to turn all the power over to me.

At the end of my own story—I hadn't even got to the tale yet—I saw with some satisfaction that I'd started a fight between the summoner and the friar. I don't know if they were vying for me in a decayed version of two rams bashing their heads together, but they rose in their stirrups, hurling insults at each other and vowing revenge. Finally my dear Harry intervened, and settled them down.

"Peace!" cried he, "and let the woman tell her tale. You're acting like a pair of drunks" (probably not far off the mark). And turning his sweet smile on me, he said, "Please, dame Alison, do proceed with your tale." I was glad of that smile. I hadn't wanted to lose Harry's affection, though I understood he didn't want anyone to know of our night together—it would undermine his authority as our leader, and, more important, he was terrified that the dread Goodelief would hear of it and make his life even more miserable. As for me, I knew it was time to move on and, to tell the truth, some of my mocking use of clerical logic had been directed at Troilus. Rather than trying to compete with the miller, I'd decided to tell a tale that would surprise my comrades, a mix of magic and morality.

Long ago, in King Arthur's time, when fairy-folk still abounded, a knight, out hunting, meets a solitary maid. The knight decides he will have his way with her, taking her by force. He is condemned to death for his crime, but the ladies of the court beg Arthur for the knight's life; he has a chance to save himself if, in a year's time, he can discover what it is that women most desire. If he fails, he will lose his head. So on his quest he travels far and wide, everywhere receiving different answers to his question. Some say we women want wealth, others honour, others pleasure abed and still others the freedom to do as we like. Each time he asks he gets a different answer, and as the year draws to a close he is close to giving up. He turns back towards

Arthur's court, believing that he must soon die.

Passing by a forest he sees a company of dancing ladies, but as he approaches, hoping for enlightenment, they vanish, as if by magic. In their stead he finds an old woman, as ugly as any he's ever seen. She blocks his path, saying, "You cannot pass this way, sir knight. Tell me, what is it that you seek? Perhaps I can assist you. We old folk do know so much." And so he explains his plight.

"If I cannot find what it is that women most desire, I am as good as dead. But if you can help me, I will reward you well."

"Swear to me," she replies, "that you will do the next thing I ask of you and, in return, I will give you the answer you seek." He readily agrees.

"Then," says she, "I can assure you that your life is safe." She whispers her wisdom in his ear, bids him be glad, and have no fear. "You'll see, the queen will agree with me. Even the proudest of the ladies in the court will not dare to contradict me. So let us go."

They arrive in Arthur's court. Having kept his pledge to return on the appointed day, the knight announces that he is ready to answer the queen's question. The company falls silent in anticipation.

"My dear lady," he says solemnly, "what women desire is mastery— absolute power—over their husbands and their lovers. This is your greatest desire. You may kill me if you choose, but it is so." In all the court there is no woman—wife, maid or widow—who can disagree with what he's said. He has redeemed his life.

With this up jumps the old wife, telling of how she gave the knight his answer, and of his promise to her. "Now with the court as witness, sir, I claim my reward. I ask that you take me as your wife for, as you well know, I have saved your life."

"I know what I promised," cries the knight. "Yet for the love of God, ask for something else! Take my wealth, but let my body go!"

"No," she replies, "though I am ugly, old and poor, I care for nothing on earth but to be your wife, and your love."

"My love? Rather my damnation! Alas, that anyone of my birth should be so disgraced." But his protests are for nought.

He is held to his promise and on the morrow they are wed.

All day he hides like an owl, bemoaning his fate, and great is his woe that night when they are brought to bed. But as he twists and turns, his old wife lies smiling to herself. Finally she says, "Dear husband, do other knights behave in such a way? I am your own love, and indeed your wife. I saved your life. Why are you acting in this way on our wedding night? What have I done wrong? For the love of God, tell me."

"What good would that do? You are old and ugly, and low-born! Is it any wonder I'm in such a state?"

"Is this the cause of your distress? If it is, I could soon set things right if you'd but show me a little courtesy."

And so the wife delivers a wise and gentle sermon. She explains to the knight how false is his idea of 'gentility', of high birth based on old money. In fact, nobility has nothing to do with possessions, it cannot be passed from one generation to the next. A lord's son has oft been known to act the villain and his villainy makes him nothing but a churl. True gentleness comes from God alone. "And so, dear husband," she continues, "although my kin were low-born, God may yet grant me the grace to live virtuously."

As to the charge of poverty, she points out that Jesus chose to be poor and surely no one would accuse him of leading a shameful life. Poverty is really a kind of good. It frees people from anxiety. It brings wisdom to those who bear it patiently, allowing them to know both God and themselves. It shows them who their true friends are. "Therefore, sir," she adds, "reprove me not for poverty."

"Nor," she adds, "for my age. After all, your so-called gentlemen are taught to respect their elders. And since I am, as you say, old and ugly, at least you need not worry about my being unfaithful. But I'll give you a choice: will you have me ugly and old, yet a true and humble wife, or will you have me young and fair and take your chances as to my fidelity?"

The knight worries and frets. Finally with a sigh he answers. "My lady and my love—my dear wife—I put myself in your hands. You must decide which will bring the greatest happiness to you, and to me. Whatever you want will satisfy me."

"Then, since I may choose as I wish, do I have mastery over you?"

"Yes, to be sure. It's for the best."

"Kiss me," she cried, "we're no more at odds. For in truth I shall be both to you, both fair and good. I pray that I may be as good a wife to you as ever there has been since the world began. And if I am not as fair to behold as any lady, you can do as you like with me. Lift up the curtain. See for yourself!"

The knight saw that it was so—that she was fair and young—and his heart overflowed with joy. He seized her in his arms, kissing her over and over, a thousand times. And she obliged him in all those things that would give him pleasure. Thus they lived in perfect joy to the end of their days.

I thought I should end up with a benediction of my own. "May Christ Jesus," I prayed, "send us husbands who are submissive, young and generous in bed. And may he cut short the lives of those niggardly misers who won't be governed by their wives—a plague upon them all!"

I was delighted with the way my tale had turned out. The pardoner was pale with anger; the summoner and the friar were going at it hammer-and-tongs; the lawyer and monk were in a state of shock. I turned aside, wanting to see if I could gauge Troilus' reaction, but his look was opaque, I couldn't fathom it.

What was clear was that Mme. E. was continuing in her misery, clinging to the other nun, and that Braveheart was holding his horse back, riding well behind the last pilgrim. What a pair. Did they need a nursemaid to reunite them?

ॐ

Eglentyne. If anything I felt worse after we set out from Ospringe. I glanced at the garden as we rode past, and it brought back all the beauty of last night. I supposed that was going to remain the high point of my life for as long as I lived. And for as long as I lived I'd go on feeling guilty about it. I might as well die right now. I wondered how long it would take to starve myself to death and whether God would consider that wrong too. He probably would. But how could I stand to go on living? I stayed close by Cecilia, but managed to look around for Richard. I couldn't see him, and I felt a terrible pang. Had he left? Then I saw his son trot gaily by, so I knew he must be around, but where? As far away from me as he could get, that much was clear. My heart was like lead.

That woman—the host calls her Alison—started off. I knew I should show some sort of disapproval, but just couldn't manage it. After all, was I really any better? She went on and on before she even got to her tale, boasting and showing off. It was despicable, but until yesterday hadn't I been just as bad, with all my preening and sweet smiles? What was the difference?

Her tale turned out to be an upside-down sort of thing. Instead of the knight being a hero who rescued the lady, she rescued him. And after he gave her all the power they lived happily ever after. She talked a lot about nobility and of course that made me think of Richard again, of how truly noble he was. That's why he was keeping away from me, which only made me want him more.

Then the strangest thing happened. The friar was launching into a tale about a thieving summoner, which I did not want to hear. Even though it pained me I'd rather be thinking about Richard and his goodness. Hoping for a glimpse of him, I peered out from under my wimple, which I'd pulled down to my eyebrows, even lower than Cecilia's. But who should I see riding up beside me? That woman. Alison. What could she possibly want? She rode right up and looked me straight in the face.

"Eglentyne," she said, "you look ridiculous. Put that wimple back where it belongs. God chose to give you a beautiful forehead, so why try to hide it?" I looked at her in amazement. The truth is I was having a terrible time keeping it down so far; my shoulders were up to my ears. I couldn't have spoken even if I'd known what to say.

"And for the love of God," she went on, "sit up. You look like a hunchback." I could see her point. "Do you think you're impressing anyone? You certainly don't look pious, if that's what you're after. You're just being foolish. If everyone hadn't been watching me, they would surely have been wondering what on earth was the matter with you. When they do notice they'll think you've lost a button and are trying to keep your clothes on with your chin." I stared at her some more.

"Eglentyne, for the last time, listen to me. You can't ride like that all day. You're probably starting to get cramps already." I hated to admit it, but she was right. "Sit up," she said again, "I know you are feeling terrible, but this is only making things worse." How did she know what I was feeling? I loosened my chin a little and asked her.

"Well," she replied, "It doesn't take one of the wise men to figure that out. Aside from the wimple, you're not smiling, you barely touched your breakfast, you're pale as death, and you don't even know where your dear little dogs are." She was right again. Where were Tristan and Isolde? I sat up straight as a bolt and looked wildly around. Had I left them behind at the inn?

"There, now you look a little better," she said. My wimple had slipped back to its usual place. "And don't worry, the dogs are safe. Don't you want to know who has been looking after them?" Of course I did. She waited.

"Yes," I finally said.

"Well, I'm glad you haven't forgotten them entirely. They're back there, with your friend." My friend? Did she mean Cecilia? I looked over at her.

"Oh, I don't mean her," she said, "I mean your real friend, you know, the knight." I nearly fell out of my saddle. Who was this woman? "Look behind you," she went on, "which you will now be able to do since your shoulders are no longer attached to your ears." I hesitated, but only for a moment, and then looked back. There was Richard! And running happily beside him were Tristan and Isolde!

"This miracle is easily explained," said she. "He remembered to feed them this morning." I felt a surge of joy. If he cared enough to feed my dogs, that must mean he still cared for me, at least a little. Then I quickly turned back, lowering my eyes. I didn't want her to see how much this mattered to me.

"Eglentyne," she said, "you don't need to hide from me. I *know*." What did she know? What could she possibly know? Did she have magical powers like the old woman in her tale?

"You *know*?" I whispered.

"I think it's time for us to ride by ourselves a bit," she said. "We don't need to concern your travelling companions with this." I agreed. We moved our horses onto a little path that ran along side the road.

"Yes, I know. You'll probably wonder why. It's partly because I've had some experience with the affairs of the heart, with love, and with loss. I'll confess I don't know much about guilt myself. It's a curse I've been lucky enough to escape. But I've seen it in others."

I looked at her inquiringly.

"My mother, if you must know. She was undone by it . For all I can see guilt is not a feeling that comes from God. God doesn't want us to hate ourselves. And he doesn't want us to lock ourselves up, away from life, unless of course we're drawn to it by love for him. That's different."

By now I had given up trying to resist her power. "Please," I said, "go on."

"All right, I'm not one to beat around the bush. I knew when I first saw you that the religious life was not for you. You enjoy your beauty, you like men, and you enjoy your power over them. Now your shadow, the other nun, she belongs in a convent. I'm sure she's very happy there and I'm sure God's happy to have her there.

"But your being there is some kind of a mistake. I suppose it had to do with money, or the lack of it." I nodded. "It was the same for me," she went on, "that's how I ended up with my first husband. That was some kind of a mistake as well.

"The way I see it, your life is a sort of blasphemy."

I took a sharp breath.

"Oh, I don't mean because you're not happy there. I mean because you stay there when you're not happy."

"But I've taken the vows," I stammered, "... and then, there's nowhere else for me to go. My own family wouldn't have me back. At least the convent is a home of sorts."

"Some home," she snorted. "Well, as you like. But I haven't finished yet. So, I could tell you weren't happy as a prioress—everything you did was such an act, pretending to be pious and flirting all the while. You just don't know how to be honest. I've done my share of lying, for sure, but at least I can see what I'm doing, and sometimes I can be uncommonly honest, as I'm being now.

"As a matter of fact, Eglentyne, I can hardly believe I'm saying this," she added, almost as if she were speaking to herself. "I should be enjoying your suffering. It's just not like me." She shook her head as if to bring herself back to the point and turned to me again.

"Well, it didn't take long to see that you thought the knight—what's his name?—was pretty wonderful."

"Richard," I said.

"Richard," she said. "Our king's name."

"That's just what I thought," I replied.

"It was obvious just from looking at your face while Richard was telling his tale. Then I saw you talking together on the road—and then—and *then*, I just happened to see you together in the garden."

"In the garden?" I could barely choke out the words.

"Yes, in the garden, very close, holding hands. That's all, though I wondered about the rest. But this morning, instead of two happy, rosy faces, I saw what resembled two ghosts. Richard back there looks as miserable as you do."

"Miserable?" The thought filled me with happiness. "You don't mean angry, do you? Are you sure he doesn't look angry?"

"Eglentyne, believe me, I know anger when I see it. Take a

look at yonder pardoner—now there's an angry man. That's not what Richard is feeling. I promise you he's miserable and I suppose he's miserable about you."

"I'm afraid he thinks badly of me," I ventured.

"It's more likely he feels badly over how he's acted. He thinks he should have treated you with more respect. He knows he shouldn't have been out there in the garden holding hands with you last night."

"Yes, that's what he said," I answered sadly.

"But don't you see, it all depends on what you mean by 'should' and 'shouldn't'? The rules say we women should follow orders, should keep our mouths shut, shouldn't want love, and so forth. But are they right?

"Now here's a case of two lonely people, who find each other beautiful, noble, sensitive, and what happens? They stay as far apart as they can manage, each of them eaten up by misery, fully intending to go all the way back to London without ever speaking or even looking into one another's eyes again. It's ridiculous."

"Do you really think he finds me noble and sensitive?" I asked. I was fairly confident about the beautiful part.

"I do," replied she, "and that's how I know he's in love. It suspends all powers of judgement."

I knew she meant this as a slight, but I was too happy about the words "in love" to mind.

"Alison," I asked, "are you trying to be my friend? Because you are starting to make me very happy."

"God forbid," she groaned. "But why *am* I doing this?" she seemed to be asking herself. "Harry said being on this pilgrimage changed people. Can this be what he meant?"

"Who's Harry?" I asked.

She shook her head. "Oh, an old friend," she said vaguely. "But let's get back to you and Braveh—er, Richard. Does the way you're carrying on make sense?"

"What? You mean going back to London, and not speaking? Well, when you put it that way it doesn't seem to. But Alison, what else can I do? I've already done too much. Now I have to go back to the convent. I have to spend the rest of my days pretending to be a devout prioress, thinking about him and trying not to lose my mind. If I talk to him some more, or look into his eyes"—I didn't think I needed to mention the stroking of the hair, but if there was any more of that!—"it will only make it worse. Don't you see that?"

"Of course I do. You're right." That wasn't what I'd wanted to hear her say. "But you're forgetting one thing."

"What's that?" I asked, somewhere between hope and doubt.

"You don't have to go back to the convent. He loves you, Eglentyne. Marry him. Don't go back to the convent. Just don't go back."

"Do you ... do you really think that's possible?" I wanted to believe she knew what she was talking about.

"Well, I've heard many a time of sisters running away with their lovers. I'm not so sure about the marrying part, but of course neither of you would have it any other way," she added hastily when she saw the look on my face. "I'd imagine there's a legal way out of it. Your dowry would have to be paid back, of course, but he could manage that with no trouble." I was starting to believe her, but then I had a terrible thought.

"Are you sure Richard would want this, Alison? How can I ever find out? After last night I don't even dare speak to him, let alone suggest that we get married! I'm so afraid. I'm afraid of losing him. But what will he think of me? Shouldn't he *think* that I feel guilty?" I took hold of my wimple and tugged it down over my forehead again. "The last thing I want is for him to lose respect for me."

Alison rolled her eyes. "Oh, for the love of God," she said and rode off, shaking her head.

⌁

It was obvious I was going to have to wait for the friar and the summoner to finish insulting each other before there'd be a chance

of hearing what Troilus had to say. How would I pass the time? I knew
I'd be bored silly listening to them, and thought of heading back into
the woods. But then I was seized by another idea, one that struck me
by its strangeness, but which I could not seem to resist. I decided to
talk to Eglentyne.

She and her knight were both pictures of utter misery. She
was trying to look contrite by pulling her wimple down to her
nose. He was riding farther and farther behind, his head hung
low. There was something about the absurdity of their situation
that I couldn't bear. I'd just have to take the bull—or in this case
the cow—by the horns. So I rode right up to her and told her to
stop being ridiculous. At first she wouldn't speak to me and just
stared. I got her attention soon enough by letting on that I'd
seen her and Braveheart—whose name turns out to be Richard—
in the garden.

Then, God knows why, I tried to talk to her about blasphemy
(in her case being a nun when you hate the religious life). She
was taken aback, having obviously thought I was ignorant as well
as crude and she certainly hadn't expected me to be on her side.
I could hardly believe it either. I was as surprised as she was. But
I couldn't help myself. I ended by making what I would have
thought was an obvious suggestion—for her to leave the convent,
and for the two of them to get married. She was in a quite a
fluster. What should she do? What would he think of her? And
so forth. Finally her timidity won out and she pulled her head
back under the wimple like some sort of worried turtle. I gave
up and rode away.

Or I should say, I tried to give up. I said to myself, "Oh, for
all I care let her dry up in that old convent," but the fact was I
didn't really mean it. Something uncomfortable was happening
to me. God knew I'd tried, and it hadn't worked, so why couldn't
I let it go? Had all that crying for, and with, Harry softened my
brain? Or was it that wonderful moment of truth when I was
communing with the ferns? I didn't know how I'd survive without my hard-won thick skin, but it seemed to be deserting me.
Unbelievable as it seemed, I knew I'd have to talk to Richard.

With a sigh I turned my horse and rode back to him. He was lost in a fog and didn't even notice my approach. I'd never spoken to a knight and didn't know how to begin. Then I thought of the old woman in my tale and saw how it could be done.

"Sir knight," I said, "you seem troubled. Perhaps if you tell me your problem I will be able to help you." He looked up, and didn't seem to understand who was speaking to him. "I'm Alison, and I've just been talking with your friend, Eglentyne." A light came into his eyes which was quickly extinguished by a shadow.

"Eglentyne?" he asked. "How is she? I fear I have caused her great sorrow."

"Well, yes, you have," I replied, "but not in the way you suppose."

"What can you tell me? Is there any way I can atone? The thought of having hurt her is almost more than I can bear. I came on this pilgrimage to do penence for old wrongs, and all I have done is to cause new pain...."

"...Pain to one who is dear to your heart," I finished for him. He looked at me, startled. "Do not think it was she who broke your trust. I saw the feeling between you on the first day. I saw the two of you in the garden last night, and I saw her grief this morning. It was I who approached her and told her of all I had observed. I urged her to open her heart, which she did only because she saw that I already understood. She loves you, Sir Richard, and her heart is breaking. She feels that such love is wrong, but she cannot help it. She believes that she has lost your respect and that she will have to spend the rest of her days in misery, in the convent."

Richard's eyes grew wide. "She loves me? Are you sure? I had feared that she must despise me, that she would want nothing more to do with me."

"Well, you feared wrong. To her you are the noblest, finest creature on earth. She wants nothing more than to be with you."

"Are you sure? Are you sure she is not angry?"

This sounded all too familiar. I sighed. "Yes, Richard, I am sure. And I am sure it would be the worst of all wrongs to let her go back to that convent. She has never been happy there, as you must know."

"Yes," he replied, "I do know it. And I said as much to her as well, which I should not have done." Was I going to have to give my lecture on the 'should'/'shouldn't' question again?

"Richard, whose judgment is that? To whose authority do you answer? That of man, or that of God? Certainly her bishop would (if he knew) chastize her, and order her back to the convent, where he would impose various heavy penances upon her. Finally, when her spirit was broken, he would lay his hand on her head and say 'daughter, you are forgiven'. But she would still be miserable, because she loves you. God, on the other hand, does not like such sacrifices." He looked at me in silence, waiting to hear more. These two, I thought with exasperation, really needed to be spoon-fed.

"Furthermore, Richard, you have put her in this position. You are responsible for this. You have shown her your love, and made her love you, not as one soul to another, but as woman to man. If she goes back, she will feel shamed as well as hopeless. There is only one honourable thing for you to do."

"Oh, Alison, please tell me what it is I must do?" he pleaded.

"It's clear. You must freely declare your love, offer to liberate her from her religious bonds. Ask her to be your wife. Isn't that what you would like?"

"Oh, yes!" he cried, but then was beset by doubt. "But do you really think that would be possible? Would she agree?" It struck me that if these two had been the first man and woman on earth, there would have been no Cain and Abel, no ten commandments—certainly no nativity or resurrection—the human race would have ended right then and there, before it ever got started. Fortunately God had better sense than that. I bit my tongue.

"The answer to both your questions is yes, Richard. You must speak to her and let her know what you want. Certainly there will be legal problems with the church. You will have to pay back the dowry, and I daresay things will go more smoothly if you also make a generous donation to the convent; perhaps offer a tempting sum on an annual basis. I suppose this sounds crude to you, but you must keep in mind that you are doing God's will. God does not want Eglentyne to end her life in that convent. He wants her to be your wife. He wants you two to live out your days in mutual love and happiness. Who knows," I added for good measure, "but what that's the reason he has caused your paths to cross on this pilgrimage?"

"I see now how right you are!" he exclaimed. "How cruel I have been to stay away from her so long. I must speak to her. I promise I will never forget what you have said. I will never leave her alone or unprotected again." That sounded at least moderately hopeful, though given these two something could still go wrong. He pushed his horse into a trot.

"Go with God's blessing." I called after him. They'd need it.

When I caught up with the others I was glad to discover that the summoner had almost finished his scurrilous tale—which, needless to say, was dedicated to insulting his rival...

...And so the greedy friar reaches down beneath the bed-clothes of the sick man, thinking to find some gold there. But when the poor fellow feels the friar's hand groping around his hole, he lets fly a fart greater than that of any cart-horse and before the enraged friar has a chance to take his revenge, the man's family drives him from the house....

Now in conclusion I will tell you the secret of how a fart may be divided between twelve friars. When the weather is fair, and there is no wind, let a twelve-spoked cartwheel be found. Let each friar kneel beside one of the spokes. Then have their confessor, whose belly shall be swollen with gas, set his arse at the hub of the wheel, and then cause him to let a monstrous fart. You shall see that both the sound and the smell will travel equally down each spoke—and thus may the fart be evenly shared by all twelve friars.

Well, I had to laugh at the summoner's revenge on his rival, but was just as glad to have missed the rest of his tale. At its conclusion Harry had to intervene again, as the two holy men went for each other's throats.

I suppose he wanted the next tale to be as different as possible from the unsavoury offerings of the friar and the summoner, because Harry then turned to Troilus.

"Sir clerk," he said eagerly, "I haven't heard a word from you all day. Can't you be more cheerful? This is no time to be studious. Come, tell us a story."

"Sir host," he replied, "subject as I am to your authority, I will obey." I was delighted to hear this. The timing couldn't have been better as far as I was concerned. I needed to hear his story before I could work out the details my strategy.

"The tale I will tell," he went on, "comes from an Italian poet—Francis Petrarch—who is now in his grave. May God rest his soul."

On the west coast of Italy lies a region known as Saluzzo. A high-born marquis by the name of Walter rules the land. His people love him, but there is one way in which he could please them more. They would like him to take a wife, so that when the sad time of his death comes, as it inevitably must, they will not be ruled by a stranger, but by his heir. Walter reluctantly agrees, but on one condition: he shall be the one to choose his wife himself. The people joyfully agree, but Walter does not choose from his own class, as they thought he would.

Oft times when out hunting he has noticed a fair young woman, sober of heart, who takes tender care of her poor old father. Griselda, for such is her name, fetches water in a bucket from the well. She sleeps on a hard pallet. What herbs and roots she can gather she cooks to provide their sustenance. Walter is drawn by her self-denial, her readiness to accept hardship. He announces the day of his marriage, telling no one who the bride will be—then, dressed in his splendid robes, he approaches the humble cottage. Griselda falls to her knees before him, awaiting his will—which is to speak to her father alone. He tells Janicula that he would like to be his son-in-law, and the old man, though astonished, agrees. "But," says Walter, "I must speak to Griselda as well, to be sure that, in becoming my wife, she will agree to submit herself to my rule." Griselda is called to the chamber. Outside, the folk gather, curious as to what the great marquis' business in that lowly place may be.

"Griselda," says Walter, "your father and I have agreed that I should wed you and I suppose you will consent. But first, I must ask you this: Will you promise always to obey my wishes, whether I cause you joy or sorrow; and never, by word nor by look, to complain?"

Quaking with fear, Griselda replies, "Lord, I am unworthy of the honour you have bestowed upon me. But whatever you wish, so shall I. I swear that neither in deed nor in thought shall I ever disobey you."

"This is enough, my Griselda." He goes out the door, Griselda following behind. Turning to his people, he says, "Here is my wife. Whoever loves me shall also honour her, and love her."

And so the preparations for the wedding begin....

(Now I have to say that when I realized what Troilus had chosen as his subject my heart sank. I'd heard versions of this tale from Jankyn, and it was even worse than the story of Constance. The very terms of Walter's proposal suggested the hardships to which he was going to subject his wife. What was the clerk's purpose in choosing such a tale? To show how violently he disagreed with what I'd said? To argue that women should in all things obey the will of their husbands? Could I have so misjudged him?

I felt like stopping my ears, but I was too curious. Perhaps he had a different point to make. He'd already implied that the aristocratic Walter was selfish and autocratic. Of course Griselda was a ninny to accept his terms, but how could she possibly suspect his true nature? Beautiful though she was, it was her subservience that attracted Walter, which didn't speak well of him. In an odd way Troilus almost seemed to be agreeing with me, or with the old woman in my tale, at least to this extent: being high-born was no guarantee of true nobility. And so I listened, watching his face as he spoke.)

...After the birth of their first child, Walter is taken by a desire to test his wife. (But why, interposed the clerk, should he do this? I believe it is wrong to test a wife when there is no reason, and to cause her such anguish and dread.) Walter concocts a lie, telling her that his gentlefolk are displeased with her because she is so low-born, and that since the birth of her daughter their complaints have increased. The child must be done away with. "But you must agree to this," he says. "Show me that patience you promised in the village."

And Griselda does agree. Neither in word nor in look does she appear to be distraught. "Nothing that you want can displease me," she replies. "Such is the will of my heart, and ever shall be." The marquis is gratified by her response, though he hides it well.

Walter goes to one of his men, a rough-looking fellow, and tells him he must bear away the child, saying he is going to kill it. So the daughter is snatched from her mother. The ruffian looks as if he's going to kill her on the spot. Griselda makes no complaint, only she piteously asks if she may kiss the child before she says good-bye, and consign her to God. Then she hands her back, saying, "Go, now, and fulfill my lord's command. But one thing more I ask, unless my lord forbid it. Lay my little child's body in some place where it will be safe from the beasts of the forest."

Her reaction is duly reported back to Walter, who though a little rueful, holds to his cruel purpose. The child is sent away to be secretly cared for by his sister in another town. Griselda's manner towards her lord in no way alters. She never mentions her daughter.

And so they continue until a son is born. When he is still a babe, Walter is once again moved to test his wife. (How needless, said the clerk, again interrupting his own story—but married men know no moderation when they have found such a patient creature!) Once again the child is taken, once again Griselda is above reproach in her patient submission to her lord's will, and once again the child is sent to Walter's sister.

The final test comes some years later. Walter calls Griselda to him and announces abruptly that he can no longer deny the displeasure of his people—she is too low-born—he must put her away and take another wife, and she must return to her father's house. Griselda meekly accepts his command, saying she knows she was never worthy to be his wife.

Her poor old father's heart is like to break when she comes home. Walter then has the children brought back in pomp and splendour, though of course no one in Saluzzo knows who they are. The daughter now being twelve years old, he pretends that she is to be his new wife. And he asks Griselda to come to the palace to take charge of the wedding preparations.

"You know so well how I like things to be and though your clothes are ragged, I ask that you perform your duty as best you can." By now, it comes as no surprise that Griselda complies. She arrays the halls, she prepares the bedrooms, she sets the table and she graciously welcomes Walter's guests.

"Griselda," asks Walter, "what do you think of my new wife? Is she not beautiful?"

"Yes, my lord, and may God bring you both great happiness to your lives' end. But, one thing more, pray do not torment her as you have done me. She has been tenderly brought up, and could not bear it." When Walter sees that his wife is still so patient, so free of resentment despite all her hardship, he cannot help but be moved.

"This is enough, my Griselda. You have been tried and tested as no woman before you. Now at last I am convinced of your constancy." He takes her in his arms, explains what he has done, and introduces her to her children.

There follows a piteous scene in which Griselda and her children are reunited. Overcome, she falls into a dead faint, but in her swoon she clasps them so tightly to her that they can scarce be removed. She is carried to a chamber, attendants remove her rags and dress her in a gown of gold, she is ushered back in honour to Walter's side ... and (we are supposed to believe) they all live happily ever after.

"By God's bones," cried Harry with some energy, "I'd gladly give a barrel of ale if my wife—blabbing shrew that she is—could only have heard this tale!"

But Troilus soon put a damper on his enthusiasm. "Hold on there, Bailly! Sorry to disappoint you, but Petrarch's moral is not that women should try to imitate Griselda." Harry looked a little abashed.

"No, good host," he went on, "it's rather that we all should strive to be constant in the face of adversity, when it comes from God. He never sends us more than we have the strength to bear and, after all, it's only just that he should test what he's created."

I was relieved to hear that Troilus wasn't urging wifely submission after all. Walter was obviously a monster, claiming for himself the power that belongs only to God. But even if Griselda represented the patience we ought to aspire to, her disgusting servility still stuck in my throat. I wasn't at all sure that God didn't want us to kick against the pricks now and then. But it seemed our clerk was not finished.

"And further," he went on, with mock solemnity, "for the sake of the Wife of Bath—*may God save her and all her kind*—let's leave off this earnest fare. After all, Griselda is dead, and so is her patience. Let no man be so foolish as to test his wife as Walter did, for if he does he will surely fail. And oh! ye arch-wives, never let humility silence your tongues, but always be ready with your retorts. Be fierce as the tiger. Fear not your husbands, show them no reverence, pierce their armour with your bitter eloquence, and you will see them them cower like the quail. Be yourselves light-hearted, and leave them to worry and weep and wail!"

Speechless is what I felt when he concluded, a state I've rarely been reduced to. Here was a worthy adversary, indeed. He'd turned the whole Walter-Griselda story around so as to

point it directly at me. He had shown, as I had, that being high-
born and rich has nothing to do with true nobility. He'd shown
the cruelty of which husbands are capable when they hold the
power, and the grotesqueness of a wife who agrees to put up
with it. While in his tale he'd pretended the opposite, it seemed
that he agreed with me completely. He was brilliant!

I saw that though he was trying hard to mantain his studious expression, the corners of his mouth were twitching, so I
assumed he was expecting a response from me. He'd as much as
invited it with his postscript to the "arch-wives," but I wasn't to
be had quite so easily, or should I say, so obviously. We neither
of us let on as to what we were doing, looking casually around as
we rode; but ever so gradually our horses happened to move towards each other. Finally we were riding together, side by side,
and none to soon, as the Merchant was about to launch into his
tale. We both started speaking at once.

"I think..." said he.

"Let's get..." said I.

"Why not?" said he, with a crooked smile.

"I agree," said I, laughing outright.

So, having come to an understanding, we turned our horses
off the road and though the hedge. There was a lovely little shady
path that we followed in silence for a bit.

"Do you really believe that business about constancy in the
face of adversity?" I finally asked. I was not one to keep my mouth
shut for long.

"What do you think?" he asked with his little smile.

"Well, I wondered. It hasn't exactly been the way I've lived
my life."

"So I gathered," he replied. "I like that in you. In my own
life, I've been all too likely to give up, but I've found that
Griselda's solution hasn't worked for me. It hasn't strengthened
my faith. Instead it seems to have led towards hopelessness. The
problem with Petrarch's story is that Griselda, as the type of the
suffering soul, has no moment of doubt, nothing approaching a
'dark night.' Though Petrarch meant well, his allegory is really

quite shallow. Anyone—well, take Job for instance—who was tried as she was, would have questioned God, would have asked, Why are you sending me such hardship? Even Jesus in the end asked God why he'd forsaken him. So," he went on pointedly, "Griselda may be held up to the masses as proof that they should accept their poverty and powerlessness as God's will—in this way she could be useful to the ruling classes—but she's of no use to a soul that's in true distress."

I could see that once this stream began to flow it would not easily be dammed. "As you may by now have inferred," he went on, "no, I don't particularly believe it. But there was another reason I chose that tale, and I think you have guessed what it is." He paused for breath and I took the opportunity to break in.

"You wanted to get my attention?" I asked.

"Yes, of course. More than that, Alison. I wanted to show you—though not the others—that I tend to agree with you. You made your case very well in your tale and I admired that. Your knight was a boor, and a terrible snob, and he badly needed to be educated. I only wish it were that easy for such men to be set straight. If he'd had the upper hand in his marriage, he would have been as arrogant as Walter; he'd already shown a great deal of cruelty.

"But luckily his wife had more sense than Griselda. Yes, she wanted the power in the marriage—and I could see that in making that point you were trying to rile the others—but beyond that, you were saying that if one partner in a marriage has to have the upper hand, it ought to be the woman. Despite all the slander that has been written by clerks about women—and I see you're well acquainted with it—the fact is that for the most part men are reared to covet power, and to abuse it. Women are not. They may be driven to it, by the circumstances of their lives—and you showed that clearly, too, in speaking of your own experience—but their inclination is not to abuse their position—they're more likely to use their strength in the interest of harmony, and of love."

I was flattered that he'd given such a positive hearing to my words and was impressed at his astuteness. But I didn't want things to get too abstract, or too serious.

"I'd like to thank you," I said, "but I can't do that quite properly until I know your name. Will you please be so good as to share it with me?" I saw the hint of a smile. He hesitated.

"You may not believe this," he finally replied, "but my name is Nicholas." I hardly knew whether I *could* believe him. What a strange coincidence that would be! But he looked to be in dead earnest. "Yes," he went on, noting my surprise, "wouldn't it be a most amazing instance of God moving in mysterious ways if the tale of the drunken miller should turn out to be a sign to this present-day Alison and Nicholas that they are somehow meant to be together?"

"It's an interesting notion," I replied, trying to gather my wits. "If so, we would certainly not want to disregard the divine will."

"Precisely," said Nicholas. I looked at him narrowly. Was this a joke? Again he read my expression.

"Yes, you're right, I am in part speaking in jest. After all, it's hard to see Robyn as an angelic messenger. But I'm partly serious as well. As soon as we left London it struck me that you were an extraordinary woman and what you've said today has confirmed my impression. You have a mind of your own, you're courageous, you have a fine sense of the ridiculous. You're possessed of a keen intelligence, but you don't hide it under a veneer of hypocrisy as most women do—take our prioress as a prime example—thinking that will make you more appealing to the opposite sex. And, if I may say so, I find you attractive, in an honest, earthy sort of way." I decided to take this as a compliment, and smiled in acquiesence.

He went on. "True, you don't fit the image of the fragile, helpless damsel of romance, but how boring she would be, how soon her charms would fade! I found it apt that you chose an old woman to be the heroine of your tale, because it had already struck me that when you are old you will be at least as interesting as you are now." It was a good thing he was running on like this, because I had absolutely no idea of how to respond. I was used to taking the initiative, to being in control, but he was leaving me no chance.

"Furthermore," he continued, "and maybe for me this is the single most impressive thing about you—life—or God?—has dealt you some terrible blows, but you've refused to accept them—as my poor, silly Griselda would have. You pick yourself up and figure out how to turn things back to your own advantage. I suppose what I'm trying to say is, you don't know the meaning of the word despair. You don't know how to give up." This was amazing. Here I had tried to paint myself as female vice incarnate and he'd ended up seeing more virtuous qualities in me than I'd ever dreamed of.

"Alison, I can see that you're taken aback by what I'm saying, and maybe I am exaggerating. Perhaps, if I'd had to deal with your iron will or your sharp tongue myself, my enthusiasm would be tempered, though I imagine that happens in most relationships. Not that I'd know because, to be completely truthful, I haven't had any to speak of in my own life. I suppose it appeals to me, too, that you've managed to live your life to the fullest, while I've been shut away with my books."

"Nicholas...," I managed to squeeze in.

"Yes? Oh, you're probably thinking I'm talking too much. Of course you're right. It's just that I never have the chance, you see. And these thoughts have been building up in me over the past three days. I've even had trouble concentrating on my reading in the evenings. But I should give you a chance to talk, too. You'd never guess it but I really want to hear whatever it is you have to say. I want to know more. For example, how is it that you are so well-read? Your knowledge of scripture is quite stunning. You use it to your own advantage, with almost the same skill as theologians who have spent years at university."

"You're right, Nicholas. I would like my say, eventually. But for the time being I've said enough. Just now what I'd like is to hear something that's really about *you*." Inside that scholarly breast of his there had to be at least a shred of male vanity and I wanted to appeal to it. "Why don't we stop here, beside this brook, so we can talk more easily."

"That's a grand idea, Alison," he said. "The others will be having their lunch at some alehouse or other. I'd hoped we could stay away. I have a loaf of bread here in my pack, and we can drink right from the stream. It will be almost like the Former Age—the trees will be our roof, the grass our cushion—and so forth, as you might say."

So we dismounted. The horses had a long drink themselves, and then took to grazing contentedly. Lulled by the music of the brook, we sat on the soft grass eating our crusts of bread (I was glad I'd had such a big breakfast)—and Nicholas began to tell me his own story.

જ

Eglentyne. After Alison left I was beside myself. I thought everyone must be staring at me, wondering what on earth she and I could have been talking about. Luckily Father John's head-ache still seemed to be bothering him, so he wasn't paying much attention to anything. Cecilia did cast me an odd glance, won-dering I suppose how I could have seemed so pious when we awoke, and yet so amenable towards 'that dreadful woman' an hour or so later. Maybe I could convince her that I was trying to save Alison's soul. I mumbled something about how God loves lost sheep and rejoices when they are brought back to the fold. That seemed to satisfy her, and she retreated into her usual medi-tative fog.

After a bit I heard the trot of a horse coming up behind me. My heart was in my throat. Could it be Richard? What should I do? I wished I could say a prayer asking for guidance, but I'd already pushed God's patience to the limit. I didn't dare to look around—and that foolish wimple was in the way, anyhow—but then Tristan and Isolde came frisking by, and soon after the rider came up beside me. It was indeed my beloved.

He was a little breathless. "Eglentyne," he whispered, so that

Cecilia and John could not hear, "My dear Eglentyne...." As he spoke I felt tears spring to my eyes. "Please, can you forgive me? Can you find it in your heart to talk with me one more time?"

Forgive him? What did I have to forgive him for?

"Of course, Richard," I stammered, earnestly hoping it was *not* just "one more time." We reined the horses in and fell behind my chaperones, who by now most definitely should have begun to worry about my carryings-on. I was grateful for headaches and contemplative raptures.

"Oh, thank you for being willing to hear me. I have been such a coward, so ignoble. I ought not to have spoken ... acted" (and here he blushed), " as I did last night. I hoped you knew the reason, but hoping is not enough. Eglentyne, I must tell you ... yes, I do esteem you as no other woman, but there is more. Beyond that, I love you. I hope I do not offend you when I say those words, but I love you, and ... and ... if it were possible I would ask you to be my wife."

The very sound of his voice, so low and earnest, had set me trembling, but when he spoke these words I had to clutch the saddle for support. "Are you all right, my dear?" he asked anxiously, laying his hand on my arm. That touch sent such a fire through me I was like to faint—not the feigned version I'd used so often to get my way, but the real thing.

"Please, Eglentyne, be not aggrieved. Perhaps you are offended at my words (though I pray not). Here, there's some wine in my flask. Perhaps you might...perhaps a sip or two will restore you...." I took the flask in my hand. He steadied it with his own, which was cold with distress, and laying his reins across the saddle, with his other hand offered me a silken scarf to dry my eyes.

I thought if I could not have this man I might as well die on the spot. I had to collect myself, I had to say something.

"Richard," I finally managed to choke out. "Richard, last night ... last night I spoke some words that have troubled me since, partly because I knew I should not have said them, but partly because they seemed so true. I did not sleep. I lay awake thinking of you, of us, in the garden. I knew God would be angry, that what I felt was a sacrilege. But I also knew what I felt was the truth. Richard, I too love you. If there were any way for me to leave the convent and become your wife I would do it with my whole heart."

"Thank you, my dearest—oh, thank you. If you are willing, I believe it may be possible. We must think it through. I will go to your bishop. I will explain, will offer whatever sum he thinks will suffice. Perhaps he may say our petition will have to go to Rome. So be it. We will wait." I interrupted him.

"But Richard, I can't go back there. Will I have to wait there, alone? I think that would kill me."

"No, dearest. Of course. You must not go back. I have a plan of sorts, if you will agree. Will you hear it?"

"Oh, yes, please—please tell me," I answered, desperate.

"Well, I have a sister, Margaret. She is hardly younger than I. She helped mother bring up Denis—my son—when I was off on the crusades. She's been married these many years to a fine gentleman. They have two lovely girls. In fact, I've thought perhaps Denis and the young one might be growing fond of one another. Their manor lies near the estuary in Kent, not far from Canterbury. It's a bit wild there, the wind sweeps in from the sea so. But their home is warm, and Margaret is sweet as a woman can be—excepting you, of course." I wondered why he was telling me all this, and I suppose he must have read my look, for he went on eagerly.

"The reason I'm speaking of Margaret and her home," he said, "is that I propose to take you there, with Denis, after we have said our prayers at the cathedral. She will care for you and she will ensure that no hint of a scandal shall ever threaten your good name. This I must be sure of, for this I must take full responsibility. If I put you in this vulnerable situation, I must be absolutely sure you are protected."

"You are so good, Richard," I said, still feeling weak.

"Of course I cannot stay there. I will return to my own estate, in Hampshire, after I have visited your bishop. We will have to endure a separation, but we can write to one another. It will be a sharp pain indeed to be apart, but knowing you are safe with Margaret and her family will be a comfort to me."

"But Richard," I cried, clutching his arm, "how can I bear it?"

"It will be for the best, my dearest. You must try to think of the many years we will have together. For your sake, I believe this to be the wisest course. When I bring you home as my bride, I want everyone to revere you as I do. I want you to have no doubts at having left your old life, and no fears about your new one. And I want you and Margaret to come to know one another, for next to you she is the woman dearest to me on earth."

My head was spinning. I wondered how I would fare away from the convent. I had grown so used to its ways, to the homage paid me as prioress. It was after all a very safe life. Then I thought about what it would mean to go back, and knew in my heart it was too late. I would never be able to forget Richard. I would never be able to repent. It would be a living death. He was offering me what I had always wanted—more than I had ever dreamed was possible—how could I refuse?

"Richard," I said, drying my eyes, "I must admit that I'm afraid. But I trust you. I know you will do as you say. You know so much more of the world, you will be able to manage things. We will be together at last. And I would dearly love to meet your Margaret. Perhaps from her I can learn a little of what it means to be a good wife, because more than anything I want to be the best of wives to you."

Now his eyes filled with tears. "You have given me a reason to go on living," he said gravely. "I had thought there was nothing left for me but penance and sorrow.

"One more thing, though, dearest, I fear that in making this choice you will believe you have angered God past the point of forgiveness. You must remember that to lose faith in his mercy is the worst sin of all. He must feel that, loving each other as we do, it is right for us to be together. Together, before the saint's shrine in Canterbury, we will kneel together and ask him to bless our union. He will not refuse. I am sure of it.

"Last night, when I told you of my sorry life, you told me not to blame myself. You said I'd tried to do what was right. Now I say the same to you. We both were sent—by people who did not understand, who did not care to understand—on journeys that were wrong for us. For years we tried our best, but for us they were not the way to salvation. They were not, in the end, what God willed for us. We must be grateful for having been brought together."

"Oh Richard," I said, "I do love you." It was only what I had said last night, but what a difference! Then it was despite myself—now I meant to say it, and was thrilled by a strange new sensation—the joy of speaking freely from my heart.

ॐ

I decided to keep my mouth shut, or to try, while Nicholas got going. I had an idea that he needed to talk about his past before we could move on.

"There's really not that much to tell," he began. "Aside from my name, I'm sorry to say I'm not much like that rollicking clerk in Robyn's tale. I was born in a village in Oxfordshire. My parents were poor. They cared for me, and for one another, but their life was so hard that at the end of the day it was all they could manage to crawl into bed and fall asleep. I was left much to myself. Aside from going to bed hungry, the earliest memory I have is of wanting to learn Latin. In church I'd heard the parson reading what seemed like wondrous stories from his enormous bible, but of course I couldn't understand a word. After mass one day I finally dared to ask if he would take me on as a student. He was kind enough, and agreed, probably out of pity as much as anything, for I had nothing to offer him in return. I must have cut quite a forlorn figure, barefoot as I was, skinny knees and elbows poking out through the holes in my clothes.

"It happened I was very quick, and worked my way through Genesis and Exodus in no time. Soon the village folk began to see me as gifted, but also as a little strange. Whatever hope I'd had of being accepted by the other boys was at an end. On the other hand the parson was proud of me as could be, and liked to show me off to the congregation. Before long, word reached the local squire, who thought he'd improve his chances of getting to heaven by paying my way as a student at Oxford.

"My parents were bewildered, but they could hardly say no. This seemed like a chance for their son to escape the drudgery of their life. So off I went, when I was little more than a child—I suppose I wasn't much older than you were, Alison, when you were first married. I was miserable. I missed my home terribly—you might not think it likely—there was but a dirt floor, and only a small fire, just for cooking. But I longed to be back there, to share a pot of watery porridge with my parents, to nestle under my little quilt and try to get warm as I watched the last sparks of the fire die out.

"But now, in Oxford, there were the books. Every one of them took me to new places, to new spaces in my mind. Looking back, I realize that they became my family and friends. At night, aching with loneliness, I would take one to bed with me and read until the candle burned out. Hard and square as they were, I wrapped my arms around them as I slept. I drank them in, but I never felt full. I was always eager for the next one. I turned out to be a good student, particularly in logic and philosophy. It helped that I did not spend my nights in the taverns, as most of my fellow-students did. I'd grown so gloomy that after a time they stopped asking me to join them.

"Just as I'd finished my degree, my poor father died, of exhaustion as much as anything. I went home to my mother who was quite broken down herself, and cared for her for some years, working at various odd jobs, until she too died. I was glad to be with her at the end, but to tell the truth I was otherwise pretty well drained and hopeless. I devoutly hoped my parents were together in heaven, for it did not seem that God had been anything but unjust to them in this life.

"The squire then insisted I go back to Oxford, to continue with my studies, which I agreed to readily enough. So I went to work on my degree, and was asked to do some teaching as well.

The idea of taking orders, of becoming a parson, never appealed to me. I could hardly imagine bringing a message of hope to my parishoners. Anyhow, my sponsor was pleased for me to continue at Oxford—if I distinguished myself as a scholar, so much the better—it would only serve to enhance his reputation.

"For several years I worked on a study of Aristotle, which brought me the greatest pleasure I'd known since those early days when I was learning Latin with the parson. But this past winter the old squire passed on, and his son having better things to do with his money (along the lines of horses and hounds), I was cut off. My treatise was well advanced, but far from completion. I went to work to keep myself—serving ale to the other students at the tavern—but the Oxford governors made it clear that in doing so I had disgraced the university, and so I was expelled." He paused.

"Alison, thank you for listening to this miserable litany. I suppose you can tell that I've talked to no one—about anything other than Aristotle—for years. When I learned that I had to leave Oxford I sank into a state of utter desolation. I had no family, nowhere to go, nothing to do with all the learning I'd spent so many years accumulating, no way to finish my work. Also, I had no way to keep myself unless I continued drawing ale from kegs and watching it disappear down the gullets of well-fed, well-funded undergraduates. Soon enough I found the whole business too distasteful to continue, and decided it would be best to end it all.

"This must sound odd coming from one who has just told the tale of Griselda. But there it is—in the face of my adversity I felt no acceptance, only bitterness. I wished I could punish God. One mid-winter night I went to the bridge at the end of the High Street, planning to throw myself into the icy waters below. In fact I did. But it seemed God had other plans for me, because the ice held. I landed hard on my side and had nothing to show for my grand gesture but a string of bruises.

"At this I had to laugh. Of course as soon as I laughed I felt better. I crawled to the bank and lay there shivering and laughing until the tears rolled down my scrawny cheeks. Then I realized there was one blessing God had left me with, and that was my sense of humour. I went back to the inn, poured some more beer for the students, and had a drink myself. I made a pact then with God that I would go on a pilgrimage, partly to atone for my pathetic self-pity, partly to discover whether there was in fact anything that life still held in store for me. I brought my few books with me and as soon as I reached the Tabard I re-discovered another blessing—my mind. Once again I was drawn into the glories of Aristotle.

"And then, as we started out the next day, I noticed you. Yes, glorious Alison of Bath, I noticed you. And I thought it was worth living at least until I could get to know you. You've made me laugh again. So here I am, and save me if you can!"

"I'd be delighted to try," I said warmly—his interests were dove-tailing quite nicely with mine.

"By listening to me you've already helped. Perhaps even Griselda would not have been as patient. I can't tell you how my spirits have been lifted by being able to share my sorrows with you. I suppose by now the others will be heading out towards Canterbury, but we mustn't follow them just yet. I need to hear from you. I need to know your secrets—the ones you didn't speak of this morning. First, how it is that, for a woman, you are so learnéd? Will you tell me that?"

"Nicholas, I will. You've been honest, and I'll do my best to repay you in kind. My being learnéd, as you call it, is easily explained. When my third husband realized he was going blind, he fretted that he would no longer be able to keep his accounts—and he was utterly terrified at the prospect of losing control of me. So he arranged for me to learn to read and every morning he'd have me go over the ledgers, telling him of the transactions that had transpired the day before. Then, as my skills increased, he'd have me read to him in the evenings, always being sure the door was locked and the key safely in his pocket. At some expense he secured some English books of the Old Testament, since of course neither of us knew Latin.

"I had no choice in this, really, but the strangest part is that, like you, I found a wonderful new world between those calfskin covers. I'd read him the pious bits—the ten commandments and the psalms—over and over. 'Thou shalt not commit adultery,' I repeated dutifully, though I hardly believed it. Then, after he'd dozed off, which didn't take long, I could read whatever I chose—and such adventures I found! Esther and Judith, Moses too—and how I envied Bathsheba and Delilah their power! I revelled in Kings' glorious battles, and in David's slaying of the monster Goliath. The nights were long, and I was bored. I read it through again and again. So perhaps after all I do know that old book better than your Oxford fellows!"

"I daresay you do, Alison. And how strange, as you say, that in our loneliness we both found such solace in reading the bible. But I think there is more. How is it that you know the clerks' accusations against women so well? Of course many girls are taught a few, so as to keep them in their place, but you seem familiar with the whole catalogue."

"That, too, is easily explained, dear Nicholas." I thought it time to introduce a modest endearment. "My last husband, Jankyn, was a clerk and used to read endlessly to me about the vices of women from his wretched Latin books. You've heard the story of how we agreed to burn the worst of them. As he read he'd translate for me, hoping to make me angry—indeed, counting on it, for he adored my rages. But he did not count on my memory and he read them rather too often, so I came to know them by heart. Alone, I would dwell on what I recalled and devise arguments to refute him—which I then threw back in his astonished face. It made for some lovely hot quarrels between us, but in the end we reached a truce, and had a better time for it.

"And now, my persistent inquisitor, have I answered all your questions?"

"Well, Alison, you've done a fair job. But I suspect there's still more. How is it, for example, that you are mistress of your cloth-making business? If I do not mistake me, that's even more unusual than for a woman to know her scriptures." For one who had spent his life with his nose buried in books, this Nicholas certainly had come up with some penetrating questions about my real life.

"I hope you'll pardon my curiosity, Alison," he continued with a little sideways smile. "You must realize that you're my first real flesh-and-blood contact in years. I've been holed up reading philosophy while you've been out there busily having the experiences." Oh, he was a clever one. He knew from what I'd said earlier today that I liked nothing (well almost nothing) better than talking about my exploits. But what he did not know was that this next part was what I had tried to hide, even from myself.

The weather came to my rescue. A bank of dark clouds that had gradually been massing now looked about ready to bestow their contents upon us.

"You'll have to wait for my answer, Nicholas," I said, pointing to the sky. "Right now we'd best head for shelter." We mounted quickly and trotted the horses through the hedge up to the road. Then we just let them go. This was their regular route, so they had no doubt as to where the next inn would be. But they were used to plodding along and were delighted to be given their heads. Soon we were at a full gallop, with the first big raindrops beating in our faces, running straight into the wind. It was glorious. There was no need to urge the horses on—they were neck and neck, each trying to gain the lead—it was the chance of a lifetime as far as they were concerned.

The clouds opened as we reached the inn near Boughton, and none too soon. The horses were in a lather, their sides heaving, and their riders were not much better off. None of us, it seemed, was in the habit of such wild riding. Dripping rain and sweat, we led our brave steeds into the barn, where to our surprise, we discovered the nodding nags of our fellow-travellers, who must have seen the storm coming and decided to let it pass before setting out again. I gave the stable-boy sixpence (at which his eyes grew round as saucers), bidding him rub our horses down and give them a hot mash. He agreed with alacrity.

Nicholas and I crossed over to the inn and sheltering beneath a little overhang peered through the window. No one would have guessed that the earnest pilgrims who met our gaze were the same revellers who'd been carrying on at Ospringe only last night. Solemnly and silently they sat in obedient rows round the parson, who was just launching into a sermon about contrition, confession and penance. Even Robyn the miller looked sober. I thought the poor innkeeper had the worst of the bargain, as his customers, most of whom were nursing hangovers, were trying to achieve a state of abstinent piety—one that would, however briefly, be credible to God—before reaching Canterbury.

Nicholas and I looked at one another, shook our heads and turned away without a word. Back at the barn we found the dairy—for the innkeeper kept a few cows, as well as his sheep and chickens—and sat down gratefully before a little stove. We took off our shoes and setting them beneath the stove, hung our outer garments over a chair to dry.

On the other side of the stove we saw two strange little bundles, wrapped in flannel, wiggling this way and that. We asked the dairy woman about them.

"Why, bless you, they're the orphan lambs. One's mother died giving birth. Poor thing, it was her first time. And the other's had twins and couldn't manage the both of them. We usually get one or two each spring," she said, "though it's nothing like the north where they have whole nurseries of them. They're like children to me—I love having them. And now they're stirring. Aren't they clever, the little darlings? They know I've finished my chores and it'll be time for their meal. Just watch this! Oh, I'm sorry..." she broke off, "Martha's my name. And who may you be?"

"We're Alison and Nicholas," we replied in unison. "We're here with the other pilgrims," I added, "but they're inside listening to a sermon. We'd rather be here with you. Please, show us the orphans."

"Gladly," she replied. "They're my little treasures. My own children were carried off by a fever a few winters back, and these little ones, when I get them, are all I have. Soon enough they'll be joining the rest of the flock, but for now they're my babies, so you may be sure I take the best of care of them." She rose and fetched two tiny bottles from the cupboard, filling them with milk she'd been warming on the stove. "I suppose it's silly, but I call them Rose and Daisy, and they're ever so good. Just see how they drink." Martha unwound the bundles and went to sit on her milking stool. They came right over to her, each taking one of the cloth nipples between their soft little lips. They closed their eyes in pleasure and sucked until the bottles were dry.

"There you are, my sweethearts, now go back to your beds and get warm." As if they understood her they went and curled up on their tiny blankets. "I'll wrap them up later, when they're asleep. Isn't it good of God to send them to me," she mused, as if to herself, "when I'd like to have died of grief at losing my own little ones?"

Then seeming to remember herself, she turned to us. "Now what can I do for you two? You're my guests here, I suppose. I don't have any blankets to wrap you in," she chuckled at her little joke, "though I'm glad to see you have your wet things a-drying. Would you like some milk yourselves, and mayhap an oatcake or two?"

Her saying this reminded me of how scant our lunch had been and Nicholas must have thought so too, for he answered before me.

"Martha, thank you for showing us your lambs. And yes, I do believe we would be glad to partake of such nourishment as you describe." She looked at him uncertainly.

"We'd love some milk and oatcakes," I said, providing the translation. So these were fetched. Nicholas and I shared a bowl of fresh warm milk and a plate of oatcakes that in their rich sweetness would have been the envy of the gods. We ate in silence, dipping the cakes into the milk.

"If you come back in a bit, they'll be hungry again—growing like weeds they are—and you may feed them yourselves if you like."

"Thank you, Martha," I answered, "for your hospitality, and for sharing your little ones with us. They'll be happy sheep, I'm sure, having had such a tender mother. I know you expect nothing for our fare, but here, I beg of you, take a florin. It will help you with the care of your little ones."

Her eyes grew even wider than those of the stable boy, but she did not refuse. "Since you put it that way, so graciously, I accept your gift. And thank you both. Alison and Nicholas, you're the nicest guests I've had in some time. Most folks pass through and pay no mind to us as does the work. Where would they be of a morning if they had no milk or eggs for their breakfast? I suppose they think it comes from on high. Well, I'm used to that, but you two are different. It's been a pleasure to me to watch you put away those oatcakes. They are grand, aren't they? My mother showed me how to make them just like that, sweet and a bit crunchy. It's the butter as does that. Now mind you come back when Rose and Daisy are ready for their next meal!"

We rose and left her cozy little dairy, but we did not go back to the inn. Instead, we climbed a rough wooden ladder that led to the hayloft. It was quite dark, what with the windows being so small, and the rain was beating hard on the roof. What hay we found was last year's, but there was enough to make a warm nest of sorts, into which we settled. I could see that the time had come for me to get on with my story, and somehow the lonely, gloomy setting seemed right for it.

"Nicholas," I began, "what I have to tell you is very hard, but there's something about you, about all you've told me, your being ready to trust me, that makes me want to try.

"What you said before is true. It is uncommon for a woman to be owner of a business such as mine. I'd been left something by each of my first two husbands. They were bound by law to do that much—but they'd been sure to will the lion's share and the property to their male relations.

"What happened with the third was different. Around the time he went blind, I discovered that I was with child. It may, or may not have been his, but of course I didn't mention that when

I told him. He was wild with delight, praying nightly that it would turn out to be a boy, an heir! As we sat through those dreary winter nights, with the doors locked so I could not slip away, he would clutch my arm with one hand and lay the other on my stomach, cackling with glee whenever he felt the little kicks. 'Oh, wife,' he'd say, 'did you feel that? What strong legs it has—it must be a boy! Thanks be to God that even in the midst of my affliction I've been granted such a blessing!'

"I sourly thought the the blessing was mine as well, but I knew such a notion would not fit with his idea—his *Aristotelian* idea, if I may say so, Nicholas—of paternity. I was merely the vessel, while as father (if such in fact he was) *he* was provider of the child's vital form. I put up with his foolishness, not that I'd much choice. And to tell the truth I was not sorry myself at the prospect—for all I knew I'd be locked up with this dotard for years, and any sort of distraction would be welcome.

"But as my time approached, I began to feel strange new inklings of affection for this creature I'd never seen and only knew from its movements within me. Perhaps to spite my husband I began to hope for a girl, not that I really cared, but I enjoyed thinking of 'it' as a she, a wee Alison—she had energy enough, to be sure! Some times I felt what I supposed were angry punchings at her narrow confines, but other times I could feel an excited sort of dancing, to the music of a passing minstrel, or a languid stirring in response to my voice, as I read aloud in the evenings. After my husband fell asleep (as *deo gracias* he could be counted on to do), I'd move down to the fire and, turning my belly towards its warmth, would stroke the baby's body through my own, hoping to feel what might be a tiny arm or leg sliding by beneath the surface."

I paused, remembering that sweet pleasure all too well. Now the rain began to come down harder. We settled deeper into the hay, which was a little dusty, but still held a memory of last summer's fragrance.

"Please go on, Alison," said Nicholas. "Tell me what happened next." The pounding on the roof was so loud we had to lean together so that we could hear each other. The storm was wild enough it seemed we were beseiged, cut off from the rest of the world. Sad as I was, it was lovely up there, really—we were like run-away children in hiding from our parents—the only two people on earth who mattered. I reached over for Nicholas' hand.

"Well, what happened next of course was that the baby was born. It turned out to be a boy, after all, but after I took one look at him I completely forgot about 'wee Alison'. In an instant he was the love of my life. What a beauty he was, with his round limbs and big bright eyes, and a tuft of pure red hair sticking straight up from his perfect head. My husband was in transports, needless to say. He decreed the boy should be called Lewys, after one of his uncles, but that was fine with me. He could have named him Beelzebub and I would have loved him none the less. He was baptized on the first Sunday, and right off showed how far above the other squalling, pissing, parish brats he was. He looked about him, smiling at the show; and when the holy water was poured over his head he laughed out loud. Oh, he was a brave lad, was Lewys. And how he took to the teat, guzzling and chortling as he made his meal, and going off to sleep like an angel after. None of that puking and mewling his puny fellows were given to."

I stopped again. It was so glorious to remember him, so long since I'd let myself do so. We listened to the rain for a while. Then I asked myself if I could really bear to go on with the pain of this remembering.

"Come here, Alison," Nicholas said, so quietly I could barely hear him. He put an arm around my shoulder and pulled me over to him. His gesture was so awkward I knew this must be new for him, but there was such tenderness in him that it seemed the sweetest embrace I'd ever felt, almost like a mother's. I lay my head on his chest and rested.

After awhile he said, just as quietly, "I think it will be better if you can tell me the rest."

"I will try, dear Nicholas," I replied. "During those first weeks I was more contented than I'd ever thought possible. I didn't even mind being married to that blind old fool, as long as I had my beautiful boy. My husband was happy, too, in his own way, crowing to the neighbours about his marvellous heir, obviously delighting in this apparent proof of his virility. Soon after the baptism he called in his lawyer and made everything over to the boy. I didn't mind this either. In fact, I loved the thought of my little one being wealthy and secure. Wouldn't he be the grandest man in all the shire? And wouldn't he take good care of his mother in her old age?

"No one knew how soon the end would come, but come it did, within another month. Of course we'd heard of the plague—the dread black death—but it had been some years since the last outbreak. People fooled themselves that Bath was far enough off its path to make us safe, but of course we weren't. The plague was no respecter of boundaries. Come it did, and it took its horrible toll.

No one was ready for the speed with which its victims succumbed, or how vast the grim harvest would be. Old and feeble as he was, my husband was one of the first to be struck. The swellings appeared, followed by the fateful black spots, and within two days he was gone. I would have been relieved had it not been for my fear about Lewys—babies were said to be the most vulnerable of all. My husband was wrapped in a sheet and loaded onto the wagon that trundled through the streets each night, collecting the corpses. They were dumped in a mass grave near the church, and covered with a layer of earth so the pit would be ready for the next lot on the morrow.

"Two days passed, and I began to hope. Lewys was as cheerful and greedy as ever. I began to make a plan—perhaps we could take a horse and cart and slip away from the city. I stayed up that night packing the few things we would need, some food, some warm clothes. I even got out the bible and read a few psalms. I wanted God to grant us speed.

"But before dawn I heard him cry out and my heart froze. I reached down to the cradle, lifted him up, held him to my breast, but he would not drink. I should have known right then. But I rocked him and sang to him. Oh, I sang him every lusty tavern song I could think of, not knowing any proper lullabyes, and told him he was my beautiful boy, and still he cried, and would not drink. I hugged him to me and wept and prayed, but I could not bring myself to unwrap his blankets and look for the terrible evidence. I fooled myself—perhaps it was the cabbage I had for dinner, that must have given him the gas—but still he wailed, though now more weakly, and still I clutched him to me.

"The char came in at sunrise to make up the fire. She took one look at us and fled. Not long after, the physician arrived. (He came to us because we had money, and was still hoping to collect for the useless sevices he'd rendered my husband.) He asked to see the baby but I screamed and told him I'd never let him go. 'Then do you want me to send for the priest?' he said coolly, and I knew I wanted that even less, so I loosed my arms a bit and let him pull aside the blankets. He lifted up one little arm and then I could no longer be in doubt. There was the swelling, big as a pullet's egg—no wonder he'd been crying, poor thing. Small wonder he wouldn't drink.

"I lay back down with him and held him to me. My breasts were hard with the milk he ought to have been drinking. I kept singing to him, rocking him. I lay like that for the three days it took him to die, cursing God, pleading with him to let the plague take me too. But that was not to be. I was too strong. I'd always been glad of that strength, now I hated it. Finally, they came to wrap both of us up. They thought I must have died as well. I sprang at them and they scattered.

Then I knew that whatever else I could not let Lewys go into that pit. I came up with another plan. I was wild but I was preternaturally crafty. I crept out and took the cart from the shed, pulled it back to the house. Inside, I lit a candle, rubbed the cold little body with oils, wrapped it in a soft fleece, sang him a last song. And I brought his little bells, that he'd loved so much, and an apple, though it would be awhile before he'd have the teeth to eat it. I brought a spade and I brought the psalter. I loaded this is the cart and I knew I would have to pull it myself.

Every horse for miles around had long since been commandeered.

"As I reached the outskirts I caught up with a crowd of flee-ing survivors, moaning with terror, faces black with soot from makeshift torches which belched sulphurous smoke and cast a ghastly light over the whole mad spectacle. Before them they were driving an array of half-crazed creatures which they'd loaded down with their worldly goods. Pigs and dogs squealed and yelped as they felt the lash, running every which-way. Sheep harnessed to great ox-carts were cursed and whipped as they struggled and fell in the muddy ruts of the road, eyes glazed, sides heaving. Yet, though it would have been easy to escape without their posses-sions, no one was willing to leave them behind. Who did they think would steal them while they were gone? The corpses? The ghosts? Nicholas, I tell you it was a scene from hell.

"I knew I did not belong with them. I turned, pulling my cart with its sad, light load, and went back to the walled garden behind our house. This had been another of my husband's schemes for keeping me prisoner, but now, after all, it seemed the best place for Lewys. It was April by now—the fruit trees were in bloom, as now—and the air was soft and fragrant. I chose a sheltered corner and dug a little grave. I covered the bottom with blossoms from the trees, and, still wrapped in his fleece, I laid him on them, his bells and his apple beside him. I'd thought to read him something from the psalter, but instead I set it at his little feet. Laying the earth on that book was the easiest part of the burial. But finally I did cover him, I knew I had to, I had to keep him safe from the ravens and vultures that, in ever tighten-ing circles, were closing in on this city of death. I lay on the grave, stroking the earth, whispering to him, aching for him.

"I lay there until dawn. I was cold, and bone-tired, but still very much alive. I discovered I was hungry. I rose stiffly and went back into the house. It was empty now. All the servants were dead, or had run off. There was plenty of food in the larder. I thought I would just stay there and wait the plague out. I knew it was just a matter of time until it moved on to new victims in a new city. I drew a mug of ale from the cask and cut myself a slice of cheese. I took them to bed with me, and after drinking and eating, lay back, doubting I'd ever sleep again. But I did, of course.

"When I awoke it must have been the next day, for the sun was just coming through the east window. I stayed alone for what must have been a week. I ate some, and drank a good bit more, and saw that I was going to live. I thought back to my first wedding night, and knew I had to get back that hard shell which I'd so gladly shed the moment Lewys was born.

"So that's what I worked on. I hated God, and that helped. Lewys was pushed into a tiny cell deep inside me and covered with layer upon layer of thick skin. By the end of that week I was tougher than I'd ever been. I don't think you would have liked me much if you'd met me then, Nicholas.

"The black death did pass and after a time the city began to resemble its old self. Huge numbers of people had perished, but they were mostly the old and the very young. The merchants came back, still in possession of their precious worldly goods. The stalls in the market gradually filled with new spring crops—the farmers had not been touched by the plague. Once more ale—perhaps in greater quanities than before—flowed in the taverns. Some who survived saw their escape as a sign of God's favour, and though still shaken, began to boast of it. Others, fearing the plague's return, decided to devote themselves to a life of penance, so as to ensure their safety next time; they decked themselves out in sackcloth and ashes. My mother would have loved it.

"Both lots made me sick. It was clear to me that God had no plan here, and perhaps he had no power. If he did, why would he have ever let this happen? Taking the purest—the children—and sparing all those vile cityfolk who not only escaped but returned prosperous as ever and carried on as if nothing much had changed—this could hardly be seen as an act of divine will.

"Nicholas, you said before that I didn't know the meaning of despair, but really, that's what I felt then. God had been defeated, or perhaps he just didn't care. In any event, Antichrist had won, so I thought I might as well join his ranks. I dressed myself up and ventured forth. I went about the market showing off my finery, and then I took myself to the lawyers, bringing my husband's will with me. I argued that, as his heir had died intestate, all his goods and property now were mine. Their books and papers were all a-jumble and they were most of them adle-pates at the best of times. Much as they'd have liked to they didn't have a clue as to how to refute my claims, and were forced to agree, or I should say, to surrender.... And there, Nicholas, is a very long answer to your question as to how I came to be in possession of the weaving business.

"I was good at it, as it turned out, and I prospered. It helped that for most of the past year I'd been going over the accounts every night. I knew the business inside and out, and I was very tough. I made enemies, but that was fine with me. I hated them all anyhow. I enjoyed having Mammon as my god for a time, but before long other instincts began to reassert themselves. I thought to find out what had happened to my lover. As he was young and strong, he too had survived.

"My being rich was exactly what he had hoped for, so he was happy enough to take up with me again, beguiling me with tales of how he'd missed me. Waited on by a new set of servants, we ate and drank abundantly, making frequent and pleasurable use of my dead husband's capacious bed. It was a big improvement on his garret. Before long he started talking about our marrying. I knew he was something of a scoundrel, but then, so was I. I thought we deserved each other, and soon began to come around to his way of thinking. Together we'd make a fine pair of rascals. I never thought about Lewys anymore.

"So, Nicholas, there you are. There's not much more to tell. We did marry, and it turned out to be a wretched mistake. He made free with my money—which as he pointed out was now his—gaming and whoring. He taunted me, made a fool of me and he lived far too long. He could never really hurt me—I was that tough—but once again there I was, for the fourth time, impatiently looking forward to the death of a husband.

"At last that blessed day did arrive. He was drunk, and fell beneath the wheels of a wagon. He managed it all on his own, though I would gladly have pushed him, and was gone before he had a chance at the last rites. You may believe I was pleased by that—the thought of him going post-haste to the ranks of the devil, blubbering all the way down into the fiery pit!

"Even before his funeral I'd had my eye on the village clerk. What a pair of legs he had!—but you know the rest. We did have a grand time together, though it was mostly fighting and making up, and laughing and making love. I never told Jankyn, or any-one else, for that matter, about Lewys, though to be sure I did love him and it was terrible when Jankyn died, of just such a fever as took poor Martha's children. Though I called in the doctors and showered them with gold they could not save him. Just over a year ago it was he died, and I believe I've been griev-ing for him since then. Yet talking with you has made me see that I've also been mourning Lewys for years. It's just that I had him buried so deep inside I'd lost touch with him."

Nicholas' arm was still awkwardly about my shoulders and with his other hand he gently stroked mine. We were quiet for a long time, 'til the rain seemed to quieten down a bit. Then he said, "All the Aristotle in the world would not help me in know-ing what to say to you, Alison. What you've been through makes my woes seem paltry indeed. Yet here we are. We've both sur-vived, and find—have found—ourselves together. It means more than I can say that you've been able to tell me about the baby—about Lewys. I like to think it may make a difference that you've done so.

"Now Alison..." he faltered, "dear Alison? I think it may be time for those little lambs to have another meal. Could you bring yourself to give them their milk? Or at least one of them. I'll try the other, novice that I am in the ways of motherhood. You be sure to tell me what I'm doing wrong."

I knew it would be hard for me, but I also thought Nicholas had somehow understood that if I could, it would help bring Lewys back. And now, at last, I knew that's where I wanted him, not locked deep in some cold forgotten cell, not at the bottom of a deep pit as in my dream, but in the warmth of my heart where I could cradle him in all his brave greedy sweetness.

"What a good idea, Nicholas. Yes, do let's go see those lambs." So we climbed down the old ladder and went back into the warm dairy. There we found—as if Martha had known we were coming—two little bottles, already filled and warming on the stove. The bundles were stirring, but Martha was nowhere in sight. Gently we unwapped them—though they didn't need much help, they were that hungry—and sat on the two stools our friend had set out for us. Nicholas fed Rose, who was a bit shy, but he was ever so gentle with her, and did fine. Daisy came to me—she was wonderfully eager and finished her bottle in no time. I gathered her in my arms, she gave a little bleat and licked my cheek with her small rough tongue. I wanted to hold her longer, she was so warm, and I could feel her heart beating against mine. But she grew restless and started to wiggle. I knew it was time to let go. I set her down and she scampered over to Rose. Together they capered about the dairy a bit before settling on their blankets. Martha was right—soon enough it would be grass-time for them and they'd be ready to join the flock. Well, life had a way of reasserting itself. As we moved towards the door I reached up and put my hand on Nicholas' shoulder, then slid it down to rest on his bum, which turned out to be lean and tidy, not bad for someone who'd spent most of his life reading. He smiled, and gave me a sly sideways look. It definitely was time to be moving on.

꒰

Eglentyne. Because of our late start we reached the inn at Boughton, where we were to have our midday meal, sometime in the afternoon. Richard bade me goodbye as we neared the stable, saying he hoped he could join me later. He wanted us to be together when we got our first view of Canterbury. Of course I said yes. For the moment I found I was more interested in the prospect of some food, perhaps because of my meagre breakfast, but more likely because my heart was now so light. My sleepless night and hopeless dawn were but distant memories. As I ate I tried to hide my enjoyment, but as poor Cecilia nibbled at her dry crust she could not help but notice the speed with which I cleaned my plate—and realize she'd lost her partner in penance.

As our meal was drawing to a close our host came in and announced that he could see a storm coming, and thought it best for us to wait at the inn until it had passed. We'd still be able to reach our lodgings at Canterbury by dusk. No one disagreed. Then he said, why didn't we have a tale while we waited, and turned to the parson.

"We've heard from most of the others," he said, "and now perhaps we may have a fable from you."

"A fable? No..." replied the parson, "but I'll give you a truthful tale in prose, to conclude your entertainment. And I pray that Jesus may send me the wisdom to lead you towards the glory of the heavenly city."

"Sir priest," answered the host, "the best of luck to you. Please, do share your thoughts with us."

And so the parson began. He started by telling us that the way to the new Jerusalem—salvation—begins with penitence, and how perfect penance must consist of contrition, confession and satisfaction. I expected that his words would fill me with guilt, but to my surprise I felt a glow spreading though me. The parson spoke with such gentleness, I saw that he wanted only what was best for us, what would bring each of us along our own road to peace. And I saw that my way was to be with Richard.

I looked over at Richard. His eyes were fixed on me with intense love. I could feel the power of his devotion in that gaze. We were going to become man and wife, in the eyes of God. That was not wrong. I found it within myself to smile across at him, and he looked back at me, his face radiant with joy. I was his.

Then the parson spoke to us of the ways in which despair could be overcome. "Great courage is needed against hopelessness," he said, "lest it swallow the soul. This virtue gives people the strength to undertake difficult things, of their own free will."

I knew that it would take courage for me to leave my life at the convent and begin a new one as Richard's wife, so that must be right.

"From this," the parson went on, "will follow a sense of confidence and security, and then the performance of good works, and then constancy." And to what better work could I devote myself that to that of being a good wife to Richard, and to whom could I be more constant? I recalled Richard's words of this morning, urging me to have faith in the power of God's mercy, and Alison's telling me that, unhappy as I was, my life in the convent was a sort of blasphemy. I drifted off into a sweet, peaceful sleep....

With a gentle shrug Cecilia woke me. The parson had finished, the storm had passed, and it was time for our journey to continue. The others—except for the miller, who was snoring gently in a corner—had risen and were heading out, but over his shoulder Richard was fixing me with another of his piercing looks. My heart started its fluttering again—I said a prayer of thanks to God, and was good and truly awake, ready for our journey.

Once we were on the road, Richard left me for a time. He said he thought he must speak to Father John and tell him of our plans. That seemed right to me.

When he was gone I rode alone, in a strange new state of delight. The clouds were breaking, the sun shone through. All the world seemed a-glisten with raindrops, from the wildflowers alongside the road, to the new leaves on the trees, to the gentle crests of the hills beyond. And how sweet was that breeze that caressed my cheek, bearing with it the scent of new blossoms, of liberty, of a new life. I was lulled into a state of quiet joy. I was overwhelmed by the feeling of the complete trust I felt in Richard. Never, never, had I had that sense of certainty in God's love. Well, perhaps that was my fault. But I couldn't imagine how I could possibly be any happier. I knew Richard would take care of everything. And I knew he would come back and take care of me.

Sure enough, after a time he did rejoin me, and told me of his talk with Father John.

"I have to say he was taken aback at first," said Richard. "But I assured him that my intentions were honourable, and that you would be safe in the keeping of my sister until I had secured permission for our marriage. I also promised that I would write to the bishop and make it clear that he, Father John, had in no way been lax in his protection of you on the course of the pilgrimage—any blame as to what had transpired was to be laid at my door. He was visibly relieved to hear this, and we shook hands on it. Then he wished us both well—in fact said he believed you'd be happier with me than you had ever been in the convent. So, Eglentyne, I think you may rest easy."

I thanked him with all my heart. Then I said how I'd like to hear of his early days, before the crusades, when he was a boy. So as we rode he told me of how he and Margaret had played as children. How they made a secret shelter in the woods and pretended to be Robin Hood and Maid Marian. How they tamed a crow they called Rufus, who was their advance scout, and with whose help they found a nest of orphan fox kits, which they raised by hand with food pilfered from the manor larder (Rufus always insisted on being fed first—he was particularly fond of stewed capon and custard). Naturally the little foxes were named after the Merry Men—Margaret was most attached to the sleek Will Scarlet while Little John was Richard's favourite. Those two would play-fight and then Richard would pretend to lose, to be knocked off the log-bridge just as Little John had done to Robin Hood on their first meeting. Rufus and the little foxes followed the children everywhere as they ran though the woods—outwitting the sheriff of Nottingham at every turn—but they knew enough to stay in hiding when Richard and Margaret had to go in at night. When winter came the foxes, who were grown by then, went off to sleep in their dens, but the faithful Rufus was always waiting for them whenever they got to the woods, and would call out to them as soon as he saw them coming. He never mistook others for them, and if they were with others he would keep silent. "And when spring came?" I asked. "Did the Merry Men come back?"

"Oh, yes, we did see them. They did not forget us. And of course they still liked their treats from the larder, but they were growing shy. They preferred if we would set the food down and then step away while they ate. Well, things were different for them. They were grown men and women now. They'd paired up, and were getting their dens ready for their new families. Play-time was over, though Little John was always ready to make an exception and wrestle with me—and that made me glad. I've car-ried that memory with me, thinking in my darkest times that however else I have failed, at least I am an honorary fox."

"What about the new foxes?" I asked. "Did you tame them as well?"

"Well, that was very interesting, if a bit sad. When the vix-ens disappeared to give birth we saw less and less of the fathers. Now and then they'd come for their treats, but it was really more as if they were trying to be polite. They'd sniff, and take a bite or two, and Little John would give me a bump and a nuzzle, but then they'd fade away into the woods, carrying the rest of the food back to their families. It was clear as could be they didn't want us involved with the new ones. They'd trusted us this far, but still we were human, and our kind were the enemy. They seemed to be saying that though they'd taken the risk with us, they couldn't go so far as to put their cubs in that danger. After all, it was safer to be wild. And you know, from what I've seen of the world of men, I think they were in the right."

"What happened then?" I wanted to know. I was entranced.

"The inevitable, I suppose," he answered. "My parents de-cided we were too old for such games. It was time for Margaret to begin acting like a proper lady, and I had to start my training, learning to use a sword, jousting with the quintain, that sort of thing. I thought it was grand. I'd pretend to be Theseus battling the Minotaur or the Centaurs—he'd replaced Robin Hood as my hero by then—he was the best warrior, but also a just ruler. I suppose that's why I made him the centre of my tale on the first day, though now I know that such absolute heroism is only the stuff of legend. I worked hard. I wanted to be the best of knights, and save the world—well, you've heard about that already. Once in a while, though, I would slip back to the woods for a visit with Rufus."

"Richard," I said, "when we get to the manor will you take me to the woods and show me your secret camp? Do you think we might see the grandchildren of Rufus and the Merry Men?"

"Of course, dear Eglentyne, yes, I think we might. I'd love that. And while you are with Margaret you can ask her to tell you more of our adventures. It was harder for her than for me for me to give them up. She had always to stay indoors and sit still, keep neat and clean, learn a little needlework and music. After all, the suitors would soon be coming round."

"Now that sounds familiar. From as early as I can remember my sisters were being readied for the business of catching husbands. We were never allowed to play outdoors. I watched them be dressed up and put on display, until one by one they were all married off. Of course the plan for me was different. I was to become a bride of Christ. I wasn't too happy about it, though of course no one asked me. But now, see how wonderfully things have worked out—I wouldn't have it any other way!" It had occurred to me that my sisters, the wives of merchants, would be green with envy when they learned of my marriage—to a knight!— but I thought it better not to mention this to Richard.

By now the sun was getting low. Our host rode by to tell us that we were nearing Canterbury and suddenly, there it was, in a gentle valley before us. Really, I thought it did look like a sort of heavenly city. Perhaps that's what the parson had meant. We all stopped. Everything was bathed in the light of the setting sun. The city with its bright red-roofed houses was circled by white walls, a shining river ran beside it, and all around lay meadows and orchards in full bloom. At the heart of the city we could see the cathedral, its windows gleaming like gold, and straight ahead was the west gate, with its great turrets, summoning us.

"It's beautiful, isn't it," murmured Richard. Gently he laid his hand on mine. "To think I spent all those years in far-off lands, vainly trying to get to the holy land, only to find that it's right here in England with you."

༄

Canterbury

With the setting sun warming our backs we rode through the grand west gate and into the city. Our inn, magically named "Chekkers of Hope," just suited my new state of mind and heart. The bleakness of Bath had gradually fallen away, like last year's dry leaves. I felt as the trees must when they've just brought forth a bright new set of green buds, bursting with freshness. My day with Nicholas had a lot to do with this, but so had my night with Harry. I had to talk with him again.

Nicholas went upstairs to stow his pack, so I took the opportunity to head out to the stable, where I hoped to find Harry. And there he was, making sure the horses were all right. How typical this was of him, to be thinking of our hard-working mounts while the others were looking to their own comfort. I stood in the doorway awhile, watching him as he went from stall to stall, speaking softly to each of them, giving them a pat, some water or hay, whatever they needed.

At last I stole up behind him and put my arms around his waist. Without looking he knew who it was.

"Oh, Alison," he said, "how glad I am you've come. I've been thinking of you all day."

"Harry," I replied, my face against his great warm back, "I just had to tell you how I loved last night." He turned, and put his arms about me too, leaning down to bury his face in my hair.

"You still smell of figs," he said happily. "I hope you don't mind my having been so busy...."

"Harry, you don't need to apologize for anything. I know you have so many things to take care of. You told me how important the pilgrims are to you, how you hope that each one of us will feel better for having come to Canterbury. Well, it's been that way for me. I want you to know our time together has been a great part of that."

"Alison, I thank you for saying so. I know I will never forget you." He hugged me harder. I knew Harry had had the night of his life with me, but also that he was a little nervous as to my expectations. His position as our leader was, in the long run, what was most important to him, and Goodlief cast a very long shadow.

"You know, Harry," I said, wanting to let him off, but also wanting to be free myself, "last night was so grand I doubt we could ever match it again. Shall we let it go at that, then, and always be glad of the joy we had together?" I did not think it would be kind of me to say I knew he was afraid of his wife finding out about us.

"Why, yes, Alison, of course, if that's what you'd like." I could feel the relief going through him. I'd given him the chance to remain the gentleman by respecting my wishes. We held each other a bit longer, breathing in the sweet smell of the hay, and of each other.

At last I pulled back a bit, and saw his tears. Gently I wiped them away with the corner of my coverchief.

"It's all right, Harry," I said. "Be glad. We'll pay our respects to St. Thomas tomorrow, but it's you who got us here—that's the main thing. It makes you a saint of sorts, you know.

"But by-the-by, I have to say I feel sorry for Goodlief, missing out on all the love you have to give."

"Oh Alison," he said, choking up, "I do hate to say goodbye...."

"Harry, we'll be seeing each other in a few minutes at dinner. And every time we eat a smoky oyster we'll think of one another and smile." Now I found myself starting to feel a little weepy too, so I gave his hand a last squeeze and hurried back to the inn.

It was packed. Another lot of pilgrims had arrived from the south and the innkeeper, while gleefully rubbing his hands at his unexpected windfall, was having trouble figuring out where to put us all. It was clear I'd have to share my room with the four or five new women—if I wanted to be alone with Nicholas I'd have to come up with an alternate plan. But I wasn't worried. When the time came I was sure to figure something out.

Considering how many people there were to feed, the dinner was not bad, though the original veal stew had obviously been stretched by the last-minute addition of a few hapless and rather stringy barnyard fowl. Our group sat together, and for the most part we were a merry lot. The day's earlier solemn mood seemed to have passed. Perhaps the gentle parson's sermon had helped. Robyn and Oswald were side by side, drinking toasts to one another. While the friar and the summoner had obviously not made up, a truce of sorts seemed to be in effect. They kept their distance, making a point of enjoying the company of the monk and the pardoner, their respective allies. Len had attached himself to a buxom barmaid, who was plainly delighted by his amorous attentions.

I looked about for Eglentyne and her swain. She was with her chaperones (if such they could still be called), but Richard was sitting as near as he could respectably manage. They could hardly bear to take their eyes off each other, and took turns giving treats to her little dogs, who frolicked happily back and forth between them. So in the end they *had* been able to work things out. I felt pleased with the results of my match-making, without which Eglentyne would still be trapped inside her wimple, and Richard tangled in his wooly uncertainty. Nicholas sat with me, our legs comfortably close beneath the table. We didn't say much. There seemed to be an unspoken understanding between us that there'd be time for more communication, of various sorts, later on.

No one had mentioned the possibility of another tale, but as we got to the end of our meal the poet Geoffrey spoke up.

"Sir host," he said to Harry, "I think I was less than fair when I taxed you and the other pilgrims with the stories of Thopas and Melibee. I was having my fun, but I confess it was at your expense. Now, with your permission, I'd like to atone."

"Why of course," replied the ever-gracious Harry, though some of the others looked less than pleased at the prospect of having to sit still and listen once again. Robyn made sure his mug was filled to the brim, and Len moved stealthily towards the door. For him this interlude doubtless meant the chance for a grapple with the barmaid—no doubt he was checking to see if there was a stack of barrels handy in the hallway.

"What I'd like to do," said Geoffrey, stroking his soft white beard, "is read to you from a something I've been working on. It's a translation out of Latin—a fine bit, all about love—and there's a reason I want to share it with you just now. At the end of his tale the good parson told us of how things will be after we have taken leave of our flesh, how in heaven the blessed company will rejoice evermore in one another's joy.

"Well, not that I mean to disagree with him, of course, but it strikes me that even now, as we sit and eat and drink together, we are quite a blessed company ourselves—blest in God's grace, and in the harmony we've arrived at in the course of our pilgrimage. As I see it, it's easy enough for the angels to be free of envy, to rejoice in the happiness of others, but for us worldly creatures it's more of a challenge.

"Yet here we are, with all our differences, reflecting the glory of the creation and being glad together. What I'm trying to say, I suppose, is that it's possible for us to find God's love here on earth. More than that, it's what he wants. Heaven is fine, when the time comes, but while we're here we should not despise what he has created. We don't have to die in order to be part of his love." He stopped himself.

"Well—I don't want to try your patience, or keep you from your various enjoyments. So here it is. It's very short. It's a prayer of sorts, which I offer at the conclusion of our meal. I hope you'll like it as much as I do:

"Oh God, maker of heaven and earth," he began, "though you are yourself without change, you place all things in motion...."

"Alison, you're going to like this, " whispered Nicholas. "It's from Boethius."

"Who?" I whispered back.

"Boethius, you know, the old Roman, falsely accused. He wrote this to console himself while he was in prison, trying to figure out how our world can be so unjust, and yet be part of a universe created and ordered by God. But let's listen. It's grand."

"Fairest of all," continued Geoffrey, "you have created the fair world in your own image. You decree that the parts of your creation, perfectly made, shall be perfectly ordered. You bind the elements in concord; you create souls and scatter them thoughout the universe, which carries out its changing process in peace and with faith.

"The sun brings us the shining day, the moon governs the night. The sea holds back its waves, so they shall not erode the earth. All this harmonious order is achieved by the power of love, which rules the earth and the sea and the heavens. To the sky you gave the stars, to men the earth. You clothed with bodies the souls you sent from heaven. Now love holds us together and makes the laws that bind us, whether in marriage or as true friends. May the love that rules the heavens also and always rule our souls."

Geoffrey fell silent, but his eyes were bright as he looked expectantly around him. The others were quiet too, for a bit—they'd never heard anything quite like this—this hopeful view of life and love on earth. Then one by one they started to thank him, to say how they liked his prayer, and as they began to laugh again, how much they preferred it to Thopas and Melibee.

"You were right," I said to Nicholas, "I do like the poet's prayer. I like it very much, and I think it's a good answer to the sorrow that so many of us have been carrying."

"Well," said Nicholas, "Geoffrey's mixed it up a little, trying to make his own point—but I can hardly object, since that's just what I did in my tale of Walter and Griselda. He's brought together the bits about the beauty of the creation, but he's quite right to do that. After all, it must be so, else how could it also be the product of God's will?

"You see what he's after—he wants no more quarrelling—he

believes that in its harmony the universe is like the divine, and if we feel and act with love, we will be too."

"Well," I said a little ruefully, "I have to say I wish I'd known of this Boethius fellow before. I've had such notions myself, but I thought maybe I was the only one."

"Exactly, Alison, and I'm sure that's why Geoffrey's translating his work, so people like you can read about the harmony of the creation for yourselves, and not feel alone in your perception of its beauty."

As we spoke Harry was thanking Geoffrey for his prayer, and the others were getting back to the business at hand. With Geoffrey's blessing, they seemed to be giving themselves more wholly over to the festivities, when suddenly a thunderous crashing from the hallway was heard, followed by some giggles and a spate of colourful nautical oaths.

"What could that be?" asked some. "It almost sounds like a stack of kegs falling over," said others. I knew that's just what it was. Len and the barmaid had been going at it a bit too strenuously and had toppled their fortress—well, I hoped they'd at least managed to complete their transaction before being betrayed. Given the present mood I didn't think anyone, except perhaps the innkeeper, would be inclined to judge them too harshly.

I was beginning to think the time had come to contrive an escape with Nicholas, when he turned, quite unexpectedly, and said, "I have to go upstairs for a bit—there's some important research I have to attend to." He must have seen the surprise in my face, because he gave me one of those sly half-smiles and said he wouldn't be long, and would I mind waiting.

I felt like saying that waiting was not exactly my forte. I did say, "Well, that depends...." He winked and put a finger to his lips. Was that supposed to be a kiss he was blowing me, or did he just want to shut me up? I was torn between anger and a teasing sense of excitement at what he might have in mind. I was half through another pint by the time he came back down the stairs carrying, of all things, his travelling pack! Now I was even more confused. Did he intend to woo me by reading from Aristotle? Was he planning to decamp on his own and head back to Oxford? I sat and waited, tapping my foot in exasperation, as he threaded his way through the crowd.

"All right, Alison, I'm ready now," he said brightly.

"Ready for what?" I asked, in a tone that was perilously close to being surly. Luckily he didn't notice.

"Well, awhile back I could already tell you thought it was far too crowded down here, for us, that is. Now, after a thorough inspection of the inn, I can tell you, categorically, that the rest of it is too crowded as well. Upstairs there are great mobs of pilgrims preparing to hurl themselves on St. Thomas' shrine—or tomb—or whatever it is—on the morrow. They've got out their sackcloth and all the trinkets and bits of bone and cloth they want blessed, and they're practicing their prayers, listing the various miracles they want performed—a crop blessed, an illness cured, an unfaithful spouse punished, you know what I mean."

Oh, did I ever know what he meant! Memories of my mother and her frenzied fellow penitents came flooding back. All I wanted was to escape.

"So," he went on, "it struck me that our only option was to leave. I thought that, if you agree of course, we might go back out to those beautiful orchards we passed as we came into the city."

Once again I found myself speechless. This Nicholas certainly had a way of reading my mind.

"Shall we go, madame?" he said, smiling crookedly and holding out his hand. I looked at him in wonder for a moment, and then, without a word, put my hand in his.

We went out through the door of the inn, and through the west gate, and then we were walking in the rows of blossoming fruit trees, which were silver in the moonlight. Behind us we could hear, ever more faintly, the sounds of the pilgrims' revel at the inn, but much closer were the sweet songs of the night birds and the ardent chorus of frogs making ready for their spring couplings. In the wake of the afternoon's rain the evening had turned quite warm—Nicholas kept my hand firmly in his and finally stopped beneath a huge old apple tree, with great, spreading branches.

"I noticed this grandfather-tree on the way in," he remarked casually, "and thought it might be the best spot for us to come back to." So he'd been making his plans for some time. "The rains will mostly not have penetrated its branches, so we can be dry, or at least less damp, beneath it, though we'll still be able to see some stars through the blossoms. And I thought we'd want both," he went on, "—a measure of dryness and a view of Boethius' magnificent firmament. There's also an old shepherd's cote along the road, which would be quite dry, if you'd prefer, but then we'd be indoors and couldn't see the stars. So, what do you say?"

For the life of me I didn't know how to answer.

"Alison, I hope your silence does not mean you are displeased. Perhaps you think I've planned ill, that it will be too wet for us to sit on this ample cushion of grass. But behold—now you will understand why I have brought my pack." He opened it, and from it drew forth two thick wooly quilts. "I've been afraid you think me too much the scholar, and I'll admit there's some truth to that, but I wanted you to see I was also capable of significant practicality." He lay one of the quilts down on the grass.

"Where did they come from?" I finally managed to say.

"Oh, that part was easy. In the course of my research I found the cupboard where the inn's bedding is stored and, well ... and ...I just took them. It was easy, really. I just stuffed them into my pack, which by the way no longer holds my travelling library, and came back down to meet you. I tried to manage a pillow as well, but it wouldn't fit. Still, I thought we might end up being quite comfortable out here."

"Indeed we might," I replied, and seated myself on the first of Nicholas' quilts. He sat beside me, quite close.

"Alison," he began, now a little hesitantly. "I hope I have not misread you, or the situation. In all honesty I must confess that—well, that I now find myself quite drawn to you, in different ways than those I listed when I first told you of my admiration. The feelings I have are quite strange to me. You must understand that my life has left very little room for women, well, no room really. I've had no money, no position, and in fact—but perhaps you're already aware of this—no experience. I've lived mostly in the past, and what I've known of the present has been the hard lives and deaths of my parents, and my humilating work as a labourer or a tapster. I'm afraid you will think me presumptuous...."

Finally he was at a loss for words, but now I was on familiar turf. What he wanted was crystal clear to me.

"Up to now you've been awfully good at arranging things," I said. "Perhaps it's time I took a turn. First off, the best thing will be for us to cover up with your other quilt, so we don't get chilled. Then I'd be glad for you to tell me something about the stars." He seemed a little surprised at the apparent change of subject, but I knew what I was doing. He was nervous, and we needed to get past that. He'd regain his courage if we began with one of his areas of expertise. After all, his having the chance to explain Boethius had led to the quilts and our being here in the orchard.

"I'd love that, Alison," he said, "but...."

"But yes, you're right. We'll have to lie down if we want to see the heavens properly."

"Just so," he said. And we lay down, side by side, our heads close together so I could follow his gaze. "We won't be able to see much, because of the blossoms, and the moon is so bright." Already I could feel him beginning to relax. "But there's one star that's always visible, it's the North Star, or *Stella Polaris* in Latin, it's that bright one up there," he said, pointing straight up from our toes. "It's always in the same spot—that's why sailors use it to steer their boats by at night. But if you were lost you could use it to find your way too, as long as the sky was clear, of course. So, that means our heads are south and our feet are north. If we wanted to go back to the city we'd have to head east, so (supposing we didn't know the way) we'd just have to keep Polaris on the left and we'd be sure to get there." I found myself getting interested. "The North Star is also part of a constellation," he went on, now quite chatty.

135

"A constellation?" I asked. I'd heard the word, but was a little vague.

"Well, they're really just collections of stars the people in olden times—you know, the days of Greece and Rome—gave names to. Often the names came from their stories, like Cassiopeia or Andromeda or Perseus. Do you know who they are?"

"Well, not exactly, Nicholas, but maybe you can tell me about them some day," I answered slyly. It was becoming increasingly clear (even as I admired his erudition, I delighted in the warm meeting of our thighs beneath the quilt) that my connection with Nicholas should not be limited to the few days it would take us to get back to London.

"Oh, yes, you'd be glad to hear their stories," he replied. "And actually they're easier to see in the summer. Anyway, the North Star is also the tip of the tail of the Little Bear, or *Ursa Minor*. There's a story there, too, about how he ended up in the heavens. If the moon were down you could see him better."

"Maybe later," I said.

Looking up through the boughs of the grandfather-tree I could see a vast chalky sort of band across the sky. "What's that, Nicholas?" I asked.

"Oh, that's the Milky Way, though some call it Watling Street."

"Watling Street?" I said dubiously. "That doesn't sound like a very heavenly sort of name to me."

"You're right about that, it isn't. You know the road we've been travelling, the Canterbury Road? Well, it's also known as Watling Street. It begins far up in the north of England, and angles all the way down though London to Canterbury. So the Milky Way, which crosses the heavens like a kind of road, has also been given that name. I think Boethius would have been pleased. He so liked the idea of our earth as a microcosm of the creation."

"A microcosm?" I asked.

"Yes, but perhaps that's something we should talk of later as well."

"Nicholas," I said after a moment, "I've been thinking. Is there any reason you have to go back to Oxford?"

"I'm afraid not," he replied, suddenly sad. "There's nothing for me there now, or any where else, for that matter. I certainly don't want to go back to my parents' village and have to face the taunts of my old neighbours."

"Would they taunt you?" I asked, surprised. "Why?"

"Because I've failed, of course. There always was some resentment at the favour the parson and the old squire showed me. And now, I haven't finished my treatise, and I've been expelled from the university. They'll see it as a sort of comeuppance. I suppose I'll go back to digging ditches, or drawing ale at some inn or other." He fell silent, obviously oppressed by his prospects.

"Well, Nicholas," I said after a bit, "I have another idea. How would you feel about coming back to Bath with me? I have my own house, plenty of room and plenty of money. You could stay with me, and go on with your work. Would you like that?"

He said nothing for some time. At last he said, "Alison, I wonder if you have been sent from above." That hardly seemed likely to me, but I didn't say so.

"Why is that?" is what I did say.

"Well, you're so generous and you're so intelligent, and you're so ... what's the word for it?" Several possibilities occurred to me, but "so warm" is what he settled on. I settled for that too. "But, how could I go with you? You have everything, and I have nothing to offer you."

"You're wrong there, Nicholas."

You have what is turning out to be a wonderful body, I thought, as I inched a little closer. But what I said was—and I meant this too—"there is so much you could teach me, and to be frank, there's so much we could learn together." I could almost feel him blushing next to me.

"Well, it's more than obvious what I could learn from you," he said, "but, really, what could I teach you beyond some old Greek and Roman stories?"

I had to think quickly.

"Could you teach me Latin?" I asked, hardly daring to hear his answer, for I'd been told—oh so many times—of woman's inferior intellect.

"Why, I'd love that, Alison. You're so quick we'd be through the verbs in no time." I didn't ask him what a verb was.

"Latin's grand. It's the gateway to so much knowledge. You could read the texts, and then what I'd been writing. And we could agree or disagree. I know you have some doubts about Aristotle, though maybe you'd come to like him when you got to know him better. I know I'm partial, but I'd be very respectful of your opinions. Oh, Alison, let's do it! I will go with you. I wish we could start right now!"

"As a matter of fact," I said meaningfully, "we could. I already know from what you've said that the Latin word for star is *stella*. Now what about the word for moon?"

"*Luna*," he said happily.

"And how about the word for tree?"

"*Arbor*," he said with growing excitement.

"*Stella. Luna. Arbor.* Lovely. All right, Nicholas. Now how do I say, 'hand'," I asked, pulling his out from under the quilt and laying it against my cheek.

"*Manus*," he said, after a moment.

"And lips?" I asked, bringing mine close.

"*Labiae*," he answered quietly.

"*Manus. Labiae.* Very good. And now, what about 'kiss'?" I asked, my lips next to his.

"*Basium*," he managed to say, as we shared a kiss. "Or," pulling away for a moment, "perhaps I should give you the plural of that—*basia*."

After some prolonged *basia*, during which Nicholas proved himself far more adept than he might have expected, I said,

"And now, how shall I say 'heart'?"

"*Cor*—just *cor*," he murmured, going for some more *basia*.

"*Cor*—that's lovely," I repeated, as I gently slid his *manus* inside my bodice. "Now, can you feel my *cor* beating?" I asked.

"Oh, yes, Alison, but let me be quite sure," he added, pushing his hand a little further. "It's like the music of the spheres," he said after a moment, "or as Boethius would say, *harmonia caeli*, the harmony of the heavens."

I let him feel the *harmonia caeli* awhile longer. We were very warm under the quilt. I was now distinctly aglow with that old familiar tingle. I hoped Nicholas was tingling too, and from the sound of his breathing and the pressure of his body it seemed he was.

Finally I said, "Now, how do I say, 'I want'?"

"*Volo*," he whispered, "but if by chance you wanted to say, 'I want you', it would be *te desidero*, or 'I want to be with you' would be, *esse tecum desidero*."

"I think I like that one best," I said, "*esse tecum desidero*."

"I like it very much as well. And there's another word you just might want to know sometime," he said.

"And what might that be?" I asked. I wondered if he were planning to go on with the anatomy lesson.

"*Amo*," said Nicholas shyly. "*Te amo*, Alison." Even I knew what that meant. "Now," he said, "surely it's time to move on to the next part of the lesson. The part where you teach me."

So I did. It wasn't difficult. Joyfully we twined ourselves together and commenced to swirl in a love sweet enough to mirror that of the celestial firmament turning above us. The moon must have gone down at some point, but we didn't notice.

With the dawn a little breeze came up and sent a shower of white petals over our orchard bed.

"This is like the Garden of Eden," said Nicholas, gazing in wonder around us. "Apple tree and all."

"Well, it is that beautiful," I agreed, "but there's one big advantage we have over Adam and Eve."

"I know what you're going to say," said Nicholas. "They had no knowledge of one another—biblically speaking—until they'd been driven, guiltily clutching their figleaves, out of paradise."

"Are you ever going to stop reading my mind?" I asked, grabbing his ears and giving his head a little shake. His dark curls fell down over his eyes and he looked utterly adorable.

"Not if I can help it," he said with a laugh, and wrapped his long, scholarly limbs about me once again.

ॐ